D A[illegible]

Allison Consents

Erotic Romance

First published by Mad Cat Publishing 2024

First edition

Editing by The Hayli McClain
Cover art by Melissa Royle-Guimarães

This book was professionally typeset on Reedsy.
Find out more at reedsy.com

Contents

Preface	iv
Acknowledgement	v
1 Temptation	1
2 The Lesson Maker	8
3 Middlemarch	53
4 Tie Me Up, Tie Me Down	57
5 Courage	100
6 Judging Emily	105
7 Climax	151
8 Wild Heaven	159
9 Consent	202
About the Author	205
Also by D Accord	206

Preface

Allison Consents explores consensual sexual experiences including submission, bondage and flagellation.

The core values for the women featured in these stories lay in pleasure and trust. Each woman consents to the activities she is willing to experiment with and engage in. The men respect her choices. Stopping the activity is the prerogative of the submissive woman.

The writer does not endorse or support sexual violence outside or beyond consensual adult relationships.

Acknowledgement

With sincere and grateful thanks to

Beta Readers: The Baroness, Hazel, Olivia and Melissa.

My editor: Hayli McClain, The Hayli McClain Editing Services.

Cover Design: Melissa Royal-Guimarães, writer and graphic artist.

One

Temptation

I had no idea that the woman I was about to meet for the second time would change my life.

I'd been staring into the empty mug as if it were a crystal ball, willing it to give me an answer. The bookshop cafe was unusually quiet; the August downpour meant I was one of the few to steal into town, away from the comfort of home.

I pushed the remains of my lunch around the plate and prepared to head over to the book department when I saw her: the paramedic who'd comforted and wrapped me in a blanket exactly a year ago.

'Allison, how are you doing?' She smiled warmly, her eyes searching mine.

'You have a good memory for names.' I tried to recall hers, but it was lost in the fog that had clouded my brain since my husband died.

'I'm sorry we couldn't have done more.'

I shook my head. 'You did your best.' In my mind's eye, I see myself crouching on the lawn, making futile attempts at CPR in the garden that had been Jack's pride and joy. 'Do you live in town?'

'Moved here recently. I was heading for a book-buying spree when I saw you.'

'Ah.' I nodded. 'Another reader.'

'Avid book slut,' she laughed.

'Book slut.' I smiled. 'That's a new one on me.'

Her broad grin revealed white teeth and dimpled cheeks. 'One of the myriad reasons my ex and I split.'

Out of her uniform, I realised how pretty she was. We were close in age, although I guessed she was a few years younger than my forty-two. 'I'm sorry. I'm sure splitting up is as tough to adjust to as being a widow.' I paused and gestured to the bookshelves. 'It's my turn to recommend something for the book group.'

She pulled a Harris Tweed purse from her bag. 'If you're not in a rush, how about another coffee? I'd love to know more about your book group.'

I hesitated, used to my own company. Even at work, I kept very much to myself. But her vibrancy was infectious, and I agreed to her invitation. 'Thanks, always a pleasure to chat about books. I'm sorry, I've forgotten your name though.'

'I'm not surprised, given the circumstances, how we met. I should have said, it's Heather.'

We spent the next hour chatting about authors we liked and then the state of the town, which, like so many towns across the country, was in decline. The independent bookshop cafe was one of the few treasures left.

She told me about her ex (a Frenchman) and her work as a

paramedic. She was funny, easy to talk to and a good listener. I began to open up and tell her things I hadn't even discussed with my oldest friends – not that I had close friends, or even family anymore. I wanted to quit my job, but I was afraid no one else would want my skills. I wanted to book a holiday, but I was too afraid to go alone. And my biggest fear: that years from now, I would have achieved nothing. By the time we finished the coffee, I felt as if I had known her for years.

Two days later she called to invite me for dinner. Her flat was in a cul-de-sac behind the avenue where I lived, on the west side of Lowerford. It was spacious and comfortable, with creatively up-cycled furniture. Tastefully modern in comparison to the traditional furniture Jack had bought for us. Her walls were adorned with framed film posters and photographs of different beaches in exotic locations.

I settled on one of the bar-stools at her kitchen island, watching her prep.

'I hope you like Cosmopolitans,' she said, handing me a pale, orange-coloured iced cocktail in a vintage glass. Then she returned to halving cherry tomatoes for the Greek salad.

'I don't think I've ever tried one,' I said, recalling the glasses of sherry or gin and tonics that had seemed so sophisticated after Jack and I left the church. 'That salad looks good.'

'Everything else is thanks to Messrs Marks and Spencer, I'm afraid,' she said, working her knife expertly through a cucumber. 'You managed the last couple of days, then? Did you quit your job, book a world tour or do anything mad?'

'I wish. I'm surprised I've survived the last twelve months without moments of madness taking over. I fluctuate between managing and feeling like a snowman who's had an encounter with a boiled kettle.'

Heather pulled a sad face. 'Here's to you and finding your future,' she said, raising her glass and clinking it against mine.

I savoured the meal she had prepared, enjoying the unfamiliar textures and spices. Jack had been a two veg and meat man.

The cocktail made me feel heady and I liked the sensation. Our conversation about favourite books and authors flowed freely. I soon realised that Heather was widely read, unlike me, who tended to cling to classics and the familiar.

'Have you started on any of those new books you bought?' I asked. 'I'm guilty of re-reading the same old writers, even since I joined the book group. I'm ready for a reading adventure, but probably... Oh I don't know where to start.'

Heather emptied the remains of the cocktail into our glasses. 'What type of story adventure? What would take you out of your comfort zone?'

'Something that's going to wake me up, jolt me, shock me even. I feel like I'm...' I shrugged. I didn't know how to describe what I was feeling without betraying Jack's memory. 'I still feel stuck in a marriage of convenience.'

'Well I didn't see that coming. What do you mean convenience? Did you parents arrange it, or something else?'

'Sort of both. My family was Brethren. Jack worked with my father. We met when Dad took me to the firm's Christmas Dance, because Mum was ill. Jack asked me to dance. I was seventeen, he was thirty-five. I'd left school when I was sixteen to look after Mum. Because of our beliefs, I didn't have any friends outside the church, and I wasn't allowed boyfriends, even if the boys were members of the church. My Dad liked Jack. He came to our house for dinner a few times, and after a few weeks Jack joined the church, then asked Dad if he could propose to me.

I took a breath, the personal monologue, encouraged by the cocktail, surprised me.

'My parents were thrilled. I accepted because being married would give me status – in the church, I mean. Jack was old before his time, and he wasn't romantic. His idea of a special gift was a long nightie or a box of cotton handkerchiefs. Oh, this is the cocktail talking. I shouldn't be so ungrateful. Jack was a kind man, and my parents were protective. They wanted to know I'd be looked after.' I sighed. The confession had drained me.

Heather reached her hand across the table. 'You're not being mean. It sounds like you were very young and you didn't know you had other choices. Are you still Brethren?' She smiled and pointed at the cocktail. 'Have I corrupted you?'

'No and no!' I laughed. 'When Jack and I left the church, nothing really changed, except—' I tapped the glass. '—he poured us each a drink before dinner on Sundays.'

Heather shook her head. 'When I sat with you, while we were waiting for the police and transport for Jack's body, you showed me your wedding album. I thought your marriage was a love match.'

'That's why I… I feel guilty. As I grew older, I wanted more excitement, but he was content with what we had.'

'Do you mean in the bedroom? Lingerie instead of long nighties and handkerchiefs for example?'

I laughed. 'Yeah. Jack only had two girlfriends before me and he hadn't slept with either of them. Our wedding night was a disaster. Years later even, he was uncomfortable when I suggested we go and see *Bridget Jones* and then shocked when I bought tickets for *Love Actually*. We had to leave halfway through that one.'

'Another Cosmo, or wine?'

I tapped the glass to indicate another cocktail.

Heather's eyes sparkled as she squeezed fresh lime over the alcohol mixture. After she poured the cocktails, she stared at me intently for a minute. 'You know I love nothing more than a project, and you have just given me a brilliant idea.' She reached over to the coffee table for her laptop.

'I couldn't, honestly I just couldn't,' I told her after she showed me the profile she'd created for herself on a dating site.

'You don't have to include your picture, although you get more likes if you do, and there's tons of choice. You'll just have to wade through a lot of treacle.'

I smiled. 'Thanks for the thought, but it's not for me. I'll start with books, then hopefully a new job and a holiday.'

'OK, books it is. I have some ideas for you to try. How about something to spice up your bedtime?'

Heather typed in the name of an author I'd never heard of. 'Here we go, Wendy Mount, she's got some interesting stuff. Some of it's a little dark, even for me. This one features strong independent women, who enjoy submission and mastery.'

'Mastery?'

'Not like—' she made air quotes. '—a rich man meets naive younger girl.'

I shook my head, not understanding the reference.

'*Fifty Shades.* You said you watched *Love Actually* – there's a snip about making porn in that, right?'

'It was right after that scene that Jack made me leave. You're suggesting I read porn?'

'No, erotic romance. There's a variety and it depends on

what you're into, but you did say adventure.'

'I did.' I flushed. 'Are you into mastery and submission, then?'

Heather put her head to one side and grinned. 'Cheeky! It depends on my mood and of course, what he likes.'

I realised our conversation had taken an even more candid turn. 'He who?' I dared.

'Well since the French eejit there hasn't just been one,' said Heather. 'After we split I decided I should go international.'

'What do you mean?'

'I decided to travel and have fun sex with men from as many different countries as I can,' Heather chortled raucously. 'Careful, you'll catch flies,' she said, putting her index finger under my chin as my mouth gaped wide open.

I closed my mouth and heard my phone ping.

Heather smiled. 'Let me know what you think. I've just gifted you the Kindle version of Wendy's recent book.'

I arrived home, giddy from the cocktails, and giggled when I saw my Kindle in its coy Edwardian-style floral cover sitting on the bedside table. I rushed through my bedroom routine, creaming my face without paying attention to my hair line.

'Sorry, Jack,' I whispered as I opened the Kindle with a sense of urgency and clicked on the book Heather had sent me.

I spoke the title of the first story aloud. *The Lesson Maker*, sounded dangerous, and a warm tingle of excitement grew in my tummy.

Two

The Lesson Maker

I sipped on the cool iced water and moved closer to the window. My consulting room faced west and Edinburgh was enjoying a late summer. The sun was glinting over the top of the building opposite, I could see myself reflected in the glass. I trembled, readying myself for his call, and stroked my ivory satin blouse. My nipples hardened against the soft fabric. The tight black skirt moulded around my buttocks and encased my naked mound.

I glanced at the clock on my desk. One minute to go. I put the water down and followed his instructions. I stood still as a mannequin. Keeping my face forward, I scanned the building opposite, but I couldn't see anyone. Beads of sweat formed between my skin and the satin blouse. My face was burning from the intensity of the sunlight, the anticipation, thinking about him; it made me unsteady. I moved one arm backwards and grasped the side of the desk behind me. Within seconds the phone he'd given me rang. The signal to stop.

The phone rang again.

I waited for him to speak.

'You moved,' he said, in a flat monotone, and he ended the call.

I moaned inwardly; I'd failed. I turned back to the window to see if I could find him, but all I could see was the reflection of the building I was in. I felt desperate.

Then the phone beeped with a text. *The driver is waiting for you outside. Bring the keys and your handbag, nothing else.*

My stomach leapt as desperation turned to excitement. I locked the door of my consulting room and made my way downstairs to begin my new life.

Three Weeks Earlier

The cafe was bustling with early morning commuters and tourists who were in town for the month-long Fringe Festival. I'd ordered my usual double espresso and was about to pay when the barista pointed across the cafe. 'It's paid for. That man with the blue jacket.'

I opened my mouth to protest when the woman behind me exclaimed, 'Lucky girl, he's gorgeous.'

'But I've never met him before,' I snapped, feeling the flush creep up my neck and across my face. She was right. He was gorgeous. His intense stare was disarming. I felt as if he could read my mind. What was I making such a fuss about? Where was the harm in a coffee?

The stranger tilted his head and smiled as I walked towards

him. 'Thank you,' I said holding up the coffee.

'Sorry, I didn't mean to embarrass you,' he said.

His voice was smooth like caramel. His grey-green eyes reminded me of warm tide pools. I opened my mouth, but no words came out. It wasn't even nine-thirty, and here I was behaving like a stage-struck teenager. I hadn't felt like that for years, and certainly not since Mike and I split up.

'Dr Willow Turner,' the stranger said. He leaned in towards me. 'You smell delicious, by the way.'

His familiarity was beguiling. I was sure we hadn't met before.

'Sorry, I don't mean to be rude, but how do we know each other?'

'My name's Barrie. I heard you speak at the symposium.'

'Barrie…' I paused, waiting for him to tell me his second name, trying to recall meeting him. As if I would forget his face, those eyes. The silence was unnerving, electric. 'Are you a doctor here in Edinburgh?'

His eyes searched mine, then he spoke. 'You have an interesting mind, Willow. Do you ever stop to enjoy the moment, rather than asking questions?'

I swallowed. He was right: it was a habit of mine to drown out silence, unless I was in a session with a patient. 'I, well I…' I stammered, lost for words.

'To be still, to be quiet – those are the moments when we know ourselves. When we know others. You spoke about it during your talk. The magic of silence and stillness.'

'Yes, yes of course.'

He leaned in closer. 'What time do you start to see patients?'

'Hmm, well usually about now, but this morning's patient cancelled, so I'm going to do some admin.'

'Cancel admin,' he said. 'Invite me to your office instead. I'd like to see where you work.'

I was taken aback by how forward he was being, yet something about him was mesmerizing, cutting through the carefully constructed wall I'd built around me. I was about to respond when I noticed the thin strand of brown coiled leather poking out of his jacket pocket. He slipped his arm around my waist and guided me out of the cafe.

'It's a snake whip,' he said casually, when he saw me looking down towards the coil of leather between us.

'An odd thing for Edinburgh,' I blurted. 'Aren't they usually used by cowboys and cattlemen?'

'Transferable tools are like transferable skills,' he said, and pulled me closer. I felt the coil of leather pressing into my flesh through my linen dress. 'Like the power of silence,' he whispered into my ear as we arrived at my building.

I flushed, enjoying the proximity of this stranger. My abdomen tightened; I felt a wet warmth seep from my vulva into my sensible underwear. Flustered, I moved away, but I could see he'd noticed my excitement.

'There she is,' he said, turning to face me.

I knew I wasn't going to resist when he bent down to kiss me, my linen dress no armour against his erection.

His tongue probed every area of my mouth. His arms pulled me into him, held me tight against him.

I gasped for breath, wanting him like I had never wanted a man before. I responded exigently. Not yet satisfied, I reached down – but he stepped back.

Holding me at arm's length, his left hand squeezed my right breast hard, concentrating on my response.

When I let out a sigh, he placed his right index finger on her lips. 'Lesson one.'

I frowned. 'What do you mean, lesson one?'

'That's enough for today, sweet Willow,' he said, pointing his finger as if he were a teacher scolding a recalcitrant pupil.

I reached out and caught his arm. 'How many lessons are there?'

'Oh, good, you're curious. Six to begin with. I'll call you.'

He turned before I could reply, then strode towards Princes Street.

Lesson Two

I didn't hear from him for two days. I searched the internet, looking through pictures from the symposium and professional psychology sites, trying to find some way to discover who he was or where he worked. I couldn't stop thinking about him. The way he'd excited me even before he touched me, how he'd silenced my moans after he kissed me, how his hand had squeezed my breast.

Each time there was a tap on the consulting room door, I was disappointed by the arrival of a client. When my phone rang, I begged the universe for it to be his voice on the other end. I dreamt about him and woke up wet, imagining him taking me. By the end of the third day, I knew I had to take back control. I resolved to forget all about him.

I was about to leave the office when I heard another tap on the door. I checked my diary; I'd been so distracted, I was worried I'd forgotten a late appointment. But the evening block was empty.

'Hello again,' he said casually when I opened the door. He slipped inside the consulting room before I could speak. 'That green floral dress you wore yesterday wasn't a good look. This one, however—' He moved towards me, pointing at the dark blue silk wraparound, 'That's perfect.' He ran a palm over my breasts. 'Quite perfect.'

'How did you know what I was wearing yesterday? Look, I don't know what your game is, but I…'

He stepped forward and pulled me into him. Any resistance I felt vanquished as I melted at the urgency of his tongue.

'Better,' he said.

I nodded, my stomach fluttering.

'Sit, please.' He pointed to the couch where my patients usually sat.

I was about to offer him a drink when he hushed me again by putting his finger on his lips.

'Sit, relax.' His tone was calm, seductive.

I walked over to the couch and sat.

'I like the environment you've created,' he said, gesturing at the room. 'Your patients must feel very safe with you when they're here.' He walked over to my desk and examined the leather swivel office chair where I sat to do admin and computer work.

I watched while he ran his hands over the top of the smooth varnished wood. I was a tidy worker and mindful of confidential files. The desk was completely clear save for a small clock. The computer was off to the side, on a separate table. He examined the rest of the room. The pictures on the wall, the bookshelf, and the view from the window. He glanced over at me from time to time. I felt as if he were the therapist and I had become his patient.

'Do you have plans for dinner?' he asked.

I opened my mouth to reply. Once again his finger went to

his lips. I shook my head.

He smiled. 'Good. Would you like to experience lesson two?'

I looked down and waited for him to say more, to explain what he meant. He didn't. Excited by what had happened between us when he bought me coffee, I nodded agreement.

'Grand. The only rule for all the lessons is simple: we can stop whenever you wish.' He walked over to the chair opposite, where I sat to listen to my clients. His body relaxed into the upholstery. I shivered at the building tension, relishing being in his presence.

He took off his tie and placed it on the glass coffee table. Then he pulled the snake whip out of his pocket. Slowly and meticulously, he uncoiled it and draped it along the length of the coffee table.

I shifted when I felt the evidence of my arousal. I saw him notice.

He picked up the tie and walked towards me. He placed the fabric over my eyes. His breath was hot on my neck as he fastened the tie around the back of my head. 'Lesson two is trust, Willow. Do you trust me?'

Mesmerized by him, daring myself, I nodded and took a deep breath. Standing behind me, his hands moved down the front of my body, over my dress. My nipples hardened as he pushed and moulded my breasts with his hands, squeezing them until I moaned.

He removed his hands. I remained still, waiting for him to speak.

'Walk over towards your desk and sit on the chair. You should know where it is, even with your eyes covered.'

I stood and put my hands out in front of me. I'd had the same set up for almost five years, but my sense of direction failed me, and I ended up stumbling to the floor.

'Try again. Let the sound guide you,' he said, and he cracked the whip.

I felt the leather thong brush against me. There was no sting; clearly he hadn't intended to strike me. I made it over to the desk but I couldn't find the chair. I patted my hands through the air, trying to figure out where I stood.

'Good girl. Trust your instincts, follow the sound.' He cracked the whip again.

Turning too quickly, I stumbled. The heel of my shoe caught in my dress, and I heard the silk rip. The whip cracked again. This time I felt the sting as the plaited leather caught me on my backside.

'Take off the dress, then find the chair.'

I shivered at the command and pulled on the shoestring belt of the dress to open it. The fabric slipped to the floor. I was wearing a slip, but I'd never felt more naked. I took another few steps forward and found the chair.

'Sit,' he instructed.

I lowered myself onto the leather seat, my adrenalin racing. I waited for his next instruction. I listened to him pacing, then a click as the door opened and shut.

'Wait,' I cried, 'where are you…'

I snatched off the blindfold, ran across the room and flung open the door.

He was waiting by the lift.

'Why did you leave?' I panted breathlessly

'Why didn't you stay in the chair?'

'Because I heard you leave.'

'What did I say this lesson was about?'

'Trust.'

'And what was the last thing I told you to do?'

'You told me to sit in the chair.'

'Yet, here you are, standing in the corridor in your slip.'

I looked down. 'I don't understand, why did you leave?'

'I thought you trusted me, would understand silence and waiting. I'm sorry, my mistake. This isn't for you, after all.'

'What isn't?'

He shrugged and smiled. 'What you said you wanted.'

I shook my head, trying to make sense of what had just happened. Mike – my ex – and I had had beige sex for years. Now this man, this stranger, had aroused me, persuaded me to do whatever he asked, without question, and somehow I'd messed it up. But when had I said this was what I wanted?

'Bye, Willow,' he said as the lift doors closed.

I went back inside my consulting room, picked up the torn dress, closed the blinds, then sat in the chair for an hour. I had gone from taut sexual tension to confusion and anti-climax. All I knew was that, despite my usual caution, I wanted him badly.

Reprieve

The following day I failed most of the patients I saw. I couldn't get what had happened with Barrie out of my head.

By four o'clock, I was ready to finish for the day, but I had a late client booked for an intake. I decided to go out for a coffee before they arrived and was about to leave the building when the receptionist called me over.

'Sorry, you had a do not disturb message on your line when this came in.' She smiled and handed me a large white box tied with purple ribbon. 'Is it your birthday?'

'No,' I said, and headed back upstairs. There was no note or logo to indicate where the box came from, just a printed label with my name, Dr Willow Turner. I pulled the ribbon, lifted the lid and removed the first layer of white tissue. Underneath, wrapped in another layer of tissue, was a delicate pale blue satin slip. The next layer revealed a sheer chiffon wraparound dress and a pair of silver sandals. I searched through the remaining tissue for a card, but there wasn't one.

I held up the dress and the slip. They were my exact size, but the cut and quality of the fabric was more expensive than the dress I'd torn the day before. They had to be from him. 'Why send me this and remove the labels?' I muttered. I was about to pack the garments back in the box when my phone rang.

'Don't reply now, just wear what's in the box and nothing else. Six pm at the Hilton. I'll be in the bar if you choose to come.'

'Wait, I have a client at...'

'I think you'll find your client cancelled,' he said, and rang off.

'What the hell?' I looked at my appointment system. Sure enough, the new client had cancelled. I phoned the referring agency to see if they had any information. But their system didn't have any records of the booking.

'Mess with me, not my business,' I said through gritted teeth. It had taken me several years to build the practice. I wasn't about to have anyone wreck it. 'OK mister, you want to play games, I'll play – but you're going to see the other side of me this evening.'

Despite my anger, I was torn between feeling thrilled to see him again and scared by the powerful response had to the danger offered.

I gathered up the box and took a taxi to shower at my flat. I'd have to hurry if I was going to get back to the centre of Edinburgh by six. I studied myself in the mirror. The dress fitted me beautifully: the fitted, lace-trimmed slip enhanced the cleavage of my small, round breasts. I fastened a silver pendant around my neck and then removed it. He'd said nothing else.

I thought about the night Mike had decided we should pep up our sex life. He'd asked me to dress up for him in a red corset, garter belt and black stockings. He pretended his name was Abe. I felt ridiculous, and even though I tried hard to be the caricature whore he wanted me to role-play, it was hopeless. He ended up getting drunk on the whisky he'd wanted to rub all over me, and I went to bed with a book.

I'd never left home without panties before. I thought about wearing a pair for the journey and hiding them in my bag when I arrived at the hotel, ready for what I hoped was going to happen after I gave him a piece of my mind about messing with my appointment system. But nothing I tried worked under the delicate fabric without showing.

'You look beautiful, hen,' the taxi driver said when he saw me checking myself. 'Lucky man, whoever he is.'

'Thanks,' I said, flushing.

The hotel was busy with tourists and business guests, and there were three different bars. Barrie hadn't indicated which one he'd be waiting in. I was about to go to the champagne bar when he came up behind me.

'Keep walking,' he said. He slipped his arm around my waist, then ran a hand over my butt. 'Good girl.'

I smiled, wondering what he would have said or done if I'd

worn panties. Clearly he'd been watching for me to arrive; I wouldn't have had time to dispose of them. I felt like I had just passed a test and assumed this was lesson three.

He guided me to one of the bar tables and helped me onto the stool. His hand deftly moved under the fabric of the slip when I sat down. 'Close your eyes,' he said, brushing my cheek with his lips. His hand probed between my thighs, pushing my legs open. His fingers explored me.

I was dangerously close to climaxing when he stopped. So much for the telling-off I'd planned.

'Champagne, I think,' he said, nodding to the server. He placed the fingers he'd been using to tease me on my lower lip and gently prised my mouth open. 'Lick,' he whispered in my ear as the server slowly poured the pale golden fluid into the fluted glasses in front of us. I ran my tongue across the top of his fingers and climaxed.

'Thank you,' he said as the server left. Then he clinked his glass against mine.

'Lesson three?' I asked.

He shook his head. 'No, still lesson two. My planning was off yesterday. I apologise.'

I shrugged. 'I didn't know what you expected. I've only had one serious long-term relationship and it was nothing like this at the beginning.'

'Yes, with Mike.'

'How did you know?'

'You wrote about him in your blog.'

'I didn't,' I protested.

He laughed. It isn't hard to figure out who these people are to you.'

I thought about the blog and other published materials I'd

shared online.

'How do you think I knew what you were looking for?' he asked. He pressed his mouth onto the top of my hand. 'You're a special kind of woman.'

'What I was looking for – what do you mean?'

'Well, it's not the missionary position, is it? I think you proved that tonight.' He winked and kissed me on the cheek.

I breathed in deeply. My nipples pushed against the satin slip as I sipped on the champagne. I saw him check his watch. 'Do you have to be somewhere?'

'Unfortunately yes. I've ordered a taxi for you. I'll call you later to make sure you arrive home safely,' he said, lifting my hand to his lips.

'Lesson Two is over already,' I said, confused. Leaving suddenly and needing more was unbearable. I was so turned on, I almost invited the taxi driver in to finish the job.

It was past ten when he rang. 'Did the taxi driver get lucky?' he asked.

'No, although I did think about it. It was unkind to leave me wanting you. Was that your plan? That I'd ask the driver in?'

He laughed. 'Yes, but I'm glad you didn't. Did you finish yourself?'

'No. But I will. You said Lesson Two was trust. Was it also obedience?'

'Obedience will come later. Again, I'm sorry about yesterday. Lesson Three, if you want to continue, is giving and receiving.'

'The two scenarios – I mean, what happened yesterday and tonight – felt so different.'

'I've apologised; I won't say it again.' His voice was brusque.

'I'm sorry. I didn't mean to offend you.'

'You didn't. Tomorrow, your calendar says you're free after

two.'

'Yes, but I have admin and…'

'You can always say no, when I call you tomorrow.'

I didn't like not knowing what would happen next, yet I felt as if was willing to do anything he asked. But he was right. I could always say no.

He'd clearly done his research on me. He knew about Mike, where my practice was and how to turn me on. I needed to find out more about him. I checked the workshop registration for the symposium, where he said we'd met, and the list of delegates for the conference. There was no Barrie listed. Was he lying? His elusiveness made him even more exciting.

'Some psychologist *you* are, Willow,' I said aloud, knowing I'd be warning all of my female clients away from him. He was too intoxicating. I covered my eyes with a silk scarf, remembering the tie he'd used, and satisfied myself.

Lesson Three

Barrie sent a text while I was having breakfast. *I hope you slept well. Have you decided on Lesson Three or admin?*

I smiled. I couldn't bear not seeing him. *Lesson Three,* I typed back.

Think of five questions. I'll pick you up from your office at 2.

I assumed he wanted me to make the questions meaningful. Was this what he meant by giving and receiving? It seemed tame compared to what had already happened between us.

By two o'clock, I still had no idea what I was going to ask him. If anything, I had too many questions. I paced the floor nervously, waiting for him to text or call. I'd chosen a knee-length cream linen skirt and a cerise-coloured silk blouse. It was the sort of outfit that worked for day or evening, depending on what he'd had in mind, which I assumed wasn't a nature ramble. The warm spell was over, and the sky was grey with a threatened downpour and storm warning. I jumped as my phone rang.

'I'm in a taxi. I'll be outside in five minutes.'

I checked my face and sprayed on the cologne he'd said he liked in the coffee shop. I was already aroused, anticipating his touch.

He pulled me into him as soon as I climbed in the taxi. He pushed his hand under my blouse. I saw the taxi driver glance back in the mirror.

'He's watching,' I murmured.

Barrie removed his hand. 'Sorry, mate,' he said, leaning forward towards the driver. Then he moved onto the seat opposite me and held me in his gaze.

'Does being watched bother you?'

I nodded.

'You didn't seem to mind the server watching yesterday.' He winked. 'Ask me a question.'

I shivered, recalling how I'd climaxed in the bar while the server poured the champagne. 'Should I ask it now, or when we get to wherever we're going?'

'That's your first question? Now you only have five left.'

I opened my mouth to protest, but realised I was falling into a trap. 'Question one is where did we meet? It wasn't at the symposium.'

He raised his eyebrows and looked out of the window. 'Disappointing, Willow. What if you're wrong about that?'

'Are you going to answer me?'

'Which question do you want me to answer? So far you've

asked three questions and made a statement.'

'I knew you'd do this,' I said testily.

'Do what?'

'Oh, I give up. I'm not sure I like this game.'

'Why do you keep saying yes?'

I swallowed. 'I just want to know where we first met.'

'And I already told you when I saw you at the coffee shop. We met at the symposium. Your presentation was brilliant. You were inspiring, creative and the sexiest woman there.'

'But you weren't registered. And the coffee shop – how did you know I was going to be there?'

'I *was* registered. I knew about the coffee shop from your blog.'

'But I…' Then I remembered the picture I'd posted of myself at the coffee shop. 'So you…'

He held up his hand. 'I said five questions.'

'But I didn't ask…' I protested as the taxi stopped.

'That's fifteen, please,' said the driver, offering Barrie a card reader. 'Have a good one.' He winked at Barrie before driving away.

'Eww,' I said.

'Can't blame him, though, can you?' He took my hand. 'You're exceptionally beautiful, Willow.'

I'd never thought of myself as beautiful, though I had good hair and worked out to keep myself in shape. Mike had always said I was the girl-next-door type. I thought that was why he'd bought me lingerie and makeup and asked me to dress me up like a tart. I'd had other lovers, but usually two-or-three-night flings, and the sex hadn't been outstanding. The last lover had bought me a vibrator as a goodbye birthday gift, with a card letting me know I was a nice woman, but rubbish in the bedroom. Barrie hadn't even taken me to bed since we met, yet I'd had orgasm after orgasm.

The taxi had driven us to the North Quarter, an area I didn't know.

'Anything that happens once we go inside is up to you, Willow,' Barrie said. 'You can say no at any time. Are you OK with that?'

My stomach fluttered. I nodded, wondering what he thought I might object to.

We walked behind a converted church, into a courtyard. There were steel steps leading upward to an extension with mirrored glass at the rear of the building. Barrie knocked on the blue front door of the extension. A tall man in his late thirties with a beard and a mop of dark curly hair opened the door and gestured us to enter. He wore a white apron covered in paint over black jeans and a t-shirt.

'Oh,' I said in surprise, realising we'd come to his studio.

Barrie smiled. 'Andy, meet Willow.'

Andy looked me up and down and smiled. His dark eyes reminded me of warm cocoa. 'Come on over.' He pointed to a table and chairs by the back window. 'Coffee, or something stronger?'

I looked at Barrie, and then back at Andy, trying to figure out why we'd come here.

Barrie guided me to the table. 'I had been hoping Andy would agree to paint you.'

'Yeah, man, and as I said on the phone, I don't do portraits anymore.' Andy waved his hand at the different coloured canvases leaning against the walls or set on the three easels. 'Purely abstract these days. And I'm doing alright. Sorry, Willow, no offence.'

'Oh no! I had no idea we were coming to meet you. Please don't apologise.'

Barrie laughed. 'Cool your jets, both of you. Yeah, Andy, something stronger please.'

Andy poured Barrie and himself a generous whisky each, while I opted for a glass of white wine. After some banter and a lot of teasing back and forth between the two of them, Andy agreed to let me see some of his old work.

'It's in the back,' he said, pointing. 'Behind the curtain.'

The back of the studio was staged with a chaise and several pieces of Victorian furniture. The walls were hung with portraits of women in various stages of undress. Some posed erotically while others, despite their nudity, were almost virginal. I was drawn to a painting where the model was lounging on the chaise in a cotton shift, her eyes closed, her left leg raised, partially exposing her mound.

When I walked back through the curtain, both men were still sitting at the table. I stopped at the easels to look at Andy's new work. I sensed them both studying me. 'Why the change in style?'

'I told you she's a curious woman. Always has lots of questions, but never quite the right one,' Barrie said, walking over to me. He tilted my chin up towards the skylight. 'If you're not getting your brushes out, it would be a pity to waste the afternoon, don't you think?'

'If Willow's happy with it, it would be a pleasure,' said Andy.

'Lesson Three, giving and receiving. What do you say, Willow?'

'Sure,' I said, aroused by the uncertainty of what was going to happen next and surprised by my acquiescence to the possibility that Andy might watch.

But when he took my hand, I realised he was not just a watcher. His casual nature was very attractive, and I didn't resist when he guided me to the back of the studio. I turned to look at Barrie, who nodded.

Andy pulled me into him with his left arm, his other hand between my legs, under the skirt. I gasped for breath when I felt Barrie behind me. I was physically aroused, hot, but my brain wasn't ready. I panicked.

'No, I can't, it's too…'

Both the men stepped away.

'It's OK, said Barrie, offering me his hand. 'It's too soon.'

I remained still and took a breath, remembering the night in my consulting room when Barrie told me to sit in the chair. Earlier, he'd said I was in control of whatever happened. In truth, I was afraid of what I was learning about myself. That I liked the feeling of not knowing, not having all the answers. I knew if I didn't take a risk today, I never would. And how often would a woman like me get the chance to be loved up by two extremely gorgeous men?

'I want to go on,' I whispered.

'Are you sure?' Barrie asked.

I nodded.

Neither of them spoke, and I wondered if *they'd* changed their minds about continuing. Then Andy moved towards me. He covered my eyes with a blindfold. They turned me slowly around, undressing me, then tied my wrists behind me. I moaned as they licked and kissed me, sucked on my nipples, and stroked me between my thighs, pressing fingers against my pussy and butt, before guiding me onto my knees. They bent me forward and took me at the same time. I was euphoric from the intensity of their rhythm while they shared my body between them. Soon, I could barely hold myself up.

I smiled at my earlier thought about the lesson in giving and receiving seeming tame. Was I the gift? I wondered when they were finished, my mouth and vagina full of their cream. One of them lifted me onto the chaise and covered me with a blanket. I rested until I heard Barrie's voice asking me if I wanted more wine and some sushi. Then he removed the blindfold and untied my wrists.

'There's a shower over there,' he said. 'Why don't you freshen up before we eat?'

Lesson Four

That night, my dreams were full of sex, making love, being loved. My prurient curiosity about Andy aroused, I spent several hours researching him online. Apart from his work as a professional artist, there was nothing about his personal life to be found. No images of women or stories that suggested a life beyond art, exhibitions and painting.

Before putting me in a taxi, Barrie had handed me a phone. 'It's more private. Professionally safer for you if you use this for our calls.'

The phone was in a black leather case with my initials monogrammed on the inside cover. There were no apps or features, just a number with the name Dr B Smith as a contact. 'Yeah right, you're called Smith,' I laughed, but I searched for the name, anyway. There were several Dr B Smiths, but none of them matched the one I knew.

My own online profile was limited to my professional website and a very private Instagram account which I shared with family and close friends. The blog, which Barrie had referred to, was attached to my website and covered subjects relating to psychology and counselling. I looked through the blog to see if I could find what had suggested to Barrie that I was looking to explore a sexually hedonistic experience. Then the phone he'd given me rang.

'Do you have hiking boots?'

'Yes, but I haven't worn them in a while, and…'

'Bring them and meet me at Waverley Station at eleven,' he interrupted. 'You don't work Saturdays, and your calendar is clear.'

'Wait, how do you…' But he'd already ended the call. This was the second time he'd invaded what I considered my private space. My public appointments calendar and my private calendar were kept separate, and they were both password protected. I flicked the private calendar onto the screen on my phone. The initials BS appeared on all the dates we'd met up, including today, which said L4 after his initials. How dare he? Raging against the intrusion, I went to shower. I rubbed my flesh with the soap bar as hard as I could and decided I wouldn't go. Enough was enough – I didn't like being stalked. What I'd chosen to experience yesterday went far beyond any sexual fantasy I'd ever had, and I didn't regret it.

'But I'm damned if I'll allow you to invade my privacy,' I hissed.

By the time I'd made coffee and eaten breakfast, though, the thought of seeing him again was driving me wild. I left the flat and headed towards Waverley Station.

I'd chosen green moleskin pants, two top layers and a cashmere sweater. I also packed a light waterproof jacket with the hiking boots. It wasn't cold, but apart from the boots, I had no clue about where we were going. If his plan was hiking, I didn't want to freeze for the sake of vanity.

He put his arms around me and kissed me as soon as I arrived. 'A different surprise today, just the two of us. I think you'll like it.'

I nodded, then put my head on one side.

'OK, you can ask one question,' he said. 'Or maybe I can guess what it is?'

I felt a rush of excitement when he looked at me. Why was his simple silence so erotic?

'You can guess,' I said.

'How did I see your personal calendar?' He raised his eyebrows and smiled.

'Yes, I… I was pretty angry.'

'You're right. I should have asked you.' He stroked my cheek. 'But you still came.'

I nodded, slipping my hand into his, and we made our way across the concourse.

The luxury train, which would take us north and return us to Waverley later, was straight from a film set. I giggled as Barrie slipped next to me in front of a table laden with glasses, plates and silverware. 'I hope the surprise isn't a murder mystery,' I whispered.

'Ah, one of my favourite genres,' he said.

'You like Agatha Christie?'

'Doesn't everyone? I think it's time to find out what else we have in common. Ask as many questions as you like. I promise not to tease you like I did yesterday.'

I laughed and slapped him playfully. 'OK, but I don't think asking questions really works, does it? I mean, you know a lot about me, and I like that you're showing me things that you enjoy. You've shown me that experiencing them is more fun than talking about them.'

'You're a quick study, Willow. I knew you would be. But I didn't quite expect you to be quite so brave.'

'You mean yesterday?'

'Not just yesterday – at the hotel, letting me into your consulting room.'

I swallowed. 'I had no idea that I wanted…'

He traced his finger around my lips.

I looked down, but he tilted my chin back up and stared deep into my eyes.

'Did you know who was where?' he asked, holding my face firmly with one hand while the other pushed between my thighs and opened my legs.

I closed my eyes, remembering the hands that had massaged my breasts yesterday and the feeling of the cock in my mouth. I moaned quietly as he pushed two of his fingers into my mouth. 'I want you,' I whispered.

'Patience,' he said, and pulled away.

'Is Lesson Four patience?' I asked quietly, as the train pulled out of the station and the staff began serving drinks and elegant savoury bites.

'Patience, but through suffering, endurance.'

I stared at him. 'You want me to suffer?'

'Endurance. Waiting for permission increases the experience of pleasure.'

'So far you've taught me pleasure, but you've also made me wait, so… ' I stopped. My thoughts were scrambled. 'It's difficult to explain.'

'Because you haven't mastered it fully yet. For example,

waiting until you have permission to orgasm. The pleasure of the release after enduring the wait.'

'Is that really possible?'

'Of course.'

'Why wouldn't I want to orgasm?'

He stroked my hair and fed me one of the savoury bites. 'Because waiting for me to tell you to release yourself will bring you more pleasure. Delayed gratification – isn't that what you help your clients experience?'

'True. I also encourage them to take risks. That's why I came today.'

'So you're willing to put yourself completely in my hands? Do whatever I ask you to do? Will you push yourself beyond fear, trusting me to keep you safe?'

'Yes, I will,' I said, my stomach tingling. I squeezed the top of my thighs together.

'The thought makes you want to come, doesn't it?'

I nodded.

'Let's begin then,' he said. He removed all the cutlery, food, and glasses out of my reach, then motioned for me to be silent.

I sat back and waited for him to show me what to do next. He pulled out a newspaper, served himself wine and ordered lunch from the menu. We were almost in Dundee before he finished eating. Thanks to breakfast, I wasn't hungry. Enduring the wait, watching him was oddly thrilling. Occasionally, he held a glass of water to my lips; I took a few sips. Then he asked me to open my pack. He took out the hiking boots, but left the waterproof, snacks, and my water bottle inside. Then he stowed the pack on the shelf above our seats.

'Change into your boots and leave your shoes here. We'll be coming back to the train afterwards.'

He helped me down from the train and we left the station. We walked about a mile before turning onto a track. I'd been to the woodland trail and Dundee Law previously, but this path was unfamiliar, and there was no signpost. It looked like private land.

Because of the rain, the ground was slippery; I was glad of my hiking boots.

Barrie strode ahead, his long legs agile and steady over the uneven surface. I knew I wasn't going to be able to keep up with his pace, and he didn't look around to see the growing distance between us. When I turned the corner, I saw him disappear inside a stone cottage on the right side of the fence. On the other side was a field with cattle and a barn. The cottage looked ancient, but well kept. The cattle moved away from the fence as I passed, and I stopped to listen to the sounds of nature in her glory. It was a beautiful setting, and for a moment, as I breathed in the clean air, I could imagine myself living beyond the city in a place like this. I walked closer to the house and sat on the wooden bench in front of the porch. I didn't hear Barrie come up behind me.

'Be still,' he said. This time the blindfold he used wasn't soft fabric – it was a tight leather hood pulled down over the top of my head. It covered my ears and stopped at the tip of my nose.

I felt him patting the outside of the hood to make sure it was in place. The he said, 'Take off your clothes. All of them.'

I held onto the bench. Disoriented by the tightness of the hood, I was suddenly afraid. Was this what he'd meant by pushing beyond the fear, trusting him to take care of me? I took off the sweater, tops and my bra. I could feel the wind against my flesh. I stayed sitting. The ground was sodden and muddy. I didn't want to remove my trousers, boots or socks.

'And the rest,' he instructed.

I stood up to remove the belt and unbuttoned the waistband of my trousers. I pulled them partway down my legs. I knew they wouldn't go over my boots.

'Everything, Willow. Take off everything,' he said slowly.

I examined myself, debating whether I wanted to continue or to stop, snatch off the hood, dress myself and run back to the train station. I took a long breath, and deep inside, knew I wanted this. To prove to him that I trusted him, would endure what he was asking of me.

I bent down to undo the laces of my boots and heard the crack of the snake whip. As the sting of the plaited leather landed on my exposed buttocks, I stumbled forward into the mud. My breasts and stomach were sticky as the clay attached itself to me. He used the whip again. My lower legs were still encased in my trousers, the hiking boots firmly on my feet. I tried to get up and groaned, falling back into the mud. I heard him crack the whip again and stopped moving as the leather connected with my flesh. Silent and still, conflicted by the humiliation and, at the same time, aroused as I fought my resistance.

'Remove the boots,' said Barrie.

This time I steadied myself and managed to stand. I untied the boots. I took off my socks, trousers and panties. Drops of rain pelted over my flesh and the wind whirled around me. I had no idea of the time. I stood silent and still, completely exposed to the elements.

'Walk towards me slowly.'

I put my hands out in front of me and took small, tentative steps in the direction of his voice.

'Six more steps and you'll be out of the rain. Step up,' he

commanded as I reached the porch.

I carefully felt the way with my feet.

'I'm going to wipe your feet,' he said, then you can come inside.'

Feet cleaned, he guided me into the cottage. The room was warm, and I heard the crackling of an open fire.

'I've run you a bath. You can take off the mask there. We have about two hours before we need to be back on the train. There are fresh clothes in the bedroom next to the bathroom, and food and wine in here when you're ready.'

He guided me up some stairs. I heard the bathroom door shut, and I removed the mask. I examined my face in the mirror, then submerged myself in the warm, scented bubbles and reflected on what I had allowed to happen.

'Endurance,' I whispered, and breathed deeply. I was surprised by how calm I felt, as if I'd conquered some monumental, hitherto unattainable achievement. In the bedroom, I found makeup, silk underwear, a satin blouse, a pair of black linen trousers and an invitation to a charity dinner in London.

'Wow,' I said when I came downstairs and saw the platter of savoury and sweet delicacies on a table. He was reclining on a large cream sofa, reading a newspaper. A mixed tape of bossa nova classics was playing softly in the background.

'Wow yourself. I knew that shade of pink would be perfect for you. Come, tuck in,' he said, indicating the feast. 'Red, white or champagne?'

I shrugged. 'Either or, thank you.'

'Champagne it is,' he said. He expertly popped the cork from a bottle of Tattinger while I helped myself to a plate of food. I was ravenous.

'We're booked for dinner on the train, so save space for that,' he said, handing me a glass of pale amber bubbles.

'This is your house?'

'I inherited it. Sold off the farm, but kept the cottage.'

'And if the farmer had been in the field earlier?'

'Plan B,' he said as he clinked his glass against mine.

His eyes were playful, but I wasn't sure I believed him about not performing in front of the farmer. He was too skilled, too slick not to have done that routine with someone else before me. I was suddenly jealous.

'What is it?' he asked.

'I don't know, I'm a little confused. I mean, I'm not the first woman you've brought here, right?'

'You shouldn't ask about things when you really don't want to know the answer. You're not a simpleton or a virgin. You're a thirty-three-year-old psychologist and everything that's happened between us has been because you wanted it to.'

I sipped on the champagne, avoiding his eyes.

He switched off the music and held up a bag. 'These are your clothes. Your cashmere is on the chair. I made sure it didn't get muddy. Shall we go?'

'You're sulking now?' I asked, knowing the accusation was more about me than him. My green-eyed dragon was more powerful than any whip or harness. I could feel the anger rising.

He stood, holding his hands open. 'Why are so angry all of a sudden?'

I flew at him from the couch.

He didn't resist, letting me claw at him, beating my fists against his chest, until I dissolved into tears. Then, taking my shaking body into his arms, he caressed me until I was calm.

I softened into him and felt him harden against me. I pushed up his shirt, leaning to kiss his belly. I moved down, opening his trousers, releasing his swollen cock. I teased him with my tongue. I was about to take him into my mouth when he grasped the top of my arms firmly and rolled me around onto my knees, my head facing away from him. He slapped my butt, pushed into me and rode me until I squealed with pleasure.

We'd walked back to the train hand in hand. The row and the way we'd responded to each other afterwards had brought us closer. As we ate dinner on the train, he asked me if I wanted to continue the lessons.

'What do you think, Willow?'

'You said there were six lessons. What happens after that?'

'If you get to Lesson Six and you want to continue, you'd need to give up work, just for a month.'

I frowned. 'No, that's too much to ask.'

He nodded, but his eyes were full of disappointment. 'I understand. I told you it would be up to you whether we continued or not.'

'Wait, you mean, if I don't want to continue, we'd stop now?'

He inclined his head to the side and reached for my hand. 'When I first saw you at the symposium, I knew I wanted you, to show you that I understood what you've always been looking for. When I bought you that coffee, and later, after the hotel, I wanted to ask you to become my partner. I know what I'm asking – this lifestyle – it's not for everyone.'

I studied his face. Not seeing him again would hurt, but I didn't want to give up my independence. 'Your partner?'

'I'm asking you to commit to a way of life with me. You

either want it, and me, or you don't.'

'But my work is important to me.'

'You'd still have that, after the training. You'll have everything that you have now. But you don't have to decide right away. We have two more lessons before we'd go our separate ways, if you chose to stop.'

I paused. I didn't want to stop; I was falling hard for him. But I didn't know if I wanted or felt ready for the commitment he was asking me to consider. 'Let's continue with the lessons, on the understanding I'm not ready to agree to anything more.'

He stroked my face, his fingers outlining my cheeks, my nose, my mouth. 'OK, thank you for being clear. Undo your blouse.'

We were sitting in the back of the compartment, facing away from the other passengers, while the train staff bustled past with food and libation. He stood, taking down his pack from the shelf above us, and pulled out a small box. He opened it. Inside were two tiny, silver, clover-shaped clamps connected by a chain.

I looked at him, 'Nipple clamps?'

'Yes. They'll pinch, but these aren't the really hard-core ones. This will get you used to the sensation and build up to wearing claw clamps.'

I unbuttoned my blouse.

He placed the clamps on my nipples.

I closed my eyes, adjusting to the intensity of the painful pinching sensation.

He closed my shirt, leaving the clamps in place.

When I opened my eyes, one of the train staff was clearing the table. I knew he'd seen everything. I flushed.

Barrie smiled. 'You'll have made his day,' he said, and he pushed his hand down the back of my trousers. He worked a finger slowly into my anus.

I held by breath. The unfamiliar pinching on my nipples and his finger inside my butt were too much. I groaned loudly, shaking as he finger-fucked my butt.

'Quieter,' he said. 'Hold it, don't come.'

But the sensation was too much I yelped, trying to suppress the scream as the climax shot through me.

After I arrived home, I left the front door unlocked, then showered and lay naked face down on my bed, as he'd instructed. He was coming over later to punish me for the orgasm.

When I heard him arrive, I didn't say anything, and he didn't speak. He pulled me off the bed, onto the floor. He fastened my wrists and ankles with metal cuffs, then raised my legs up towards my wrists. He connected the metal cuffs, attaching my feet and wrists to each other, and I made an involuntary groan as I felt my muscles stretch. He opened my mouth and inserted a ball gag. He strapped the leather around the back of my head and fastened it to my wrists, extending my neck upwards. The way he'd tied me in was both uncomfortable and exciting. I couldn't move, but I was aroused. If this was a punishment for the earlier orgasm, bring it on, I thought as the pressure in my abdomen grew.

He trailed the snake whip over my back, then used it to whip me, his measured strokes stinging my butt, my upper thighs and my shoulders. He hung the whip above my bed, then left the bedroom. He returned with a glass of whisky, and sat watching me.

When he finally released me, he made love to me so tenderly that I cried. Afterwards, he showed me some of the pleasure toys he'd brought with him. I gasped when he showed me the anal hook and the dildo gag.

He chuckled, then kissed me. 'You're going to love them.'

Lesson Five

The following morning, he told me he was going to be travelling for work and would be away for the next three days. I'd already scheduled some days off and closed my practice from Monday. He told me Lesson Five would happen while he was away.

'How will that work?'

'Remember I said obedience was on the list.'

'Tell me what to do,' I said, grinning.

He laughed. 'It's not quite that easy. I need to make sure that you fully understand the principles. How we serve each other, you as an obedient submissive and me as your master.'

'"Obey" is not something I'd agree to do if I married someone.'

'It's good we're not heading to the altar, then,' he said, bending in to kiss me. 'I've also ordered you a gown to wear at the dinner, but you should go for a fitting in case they need to fix anything.'

'Thanks, I think,' I said. 'I do have a…'

I stopped as he put his finger against his lips.

'That's not how it works, Willow. I thought you'd agreed to Lesson Five?'

'Right, sorry.'

He nodded. 'I'm going to shower. Go and lie on the bed, put your hands above your head and wear the mask I put in your bedside drawer. Do not touch yourself.'

I was wearing satin shorts and a camisole I had stuffed into the back of my dresser. A gift from a lover who thought, as Mike had, that sexy lingerie was a necessity every woman should own. I put on the mask and lay down on the bed as Barrie had instructed. My body was taut with excitement, ready for whatever he'd planned.

He moved onto the bed and knelt across me. He removed the camisole and shorts, then tied my hands. When he moved down the bed, he put a leather strap under my thighs and fastened it tightly around them. Then he bound my ankles.

'Put your arms down, wrists together over your stomach,' he instructed. Then he clamped my nipples and moved off the bed.

'Please,' I whispered, 'fuck me before you leave.'

'Open your mouth.'

Relieved, I obeyed, hungry to receive him – but it wasn't his cock. It was the dildo gag he'd shown me the previous night. As soon as he fastened it, I felt anxious and shook my head to let him know I wanted to stop.

'OK,' he said. He removed the gag and started to untie me.

'It's OK, I want to, put it back on,' I said. His reassurance had been enough to settle me. I trusted him.

He stroked my cheek, gagged me again, and then whispered, 'Lie still, you're perfectly safe.' He kissed the top of my head and left the room.

I knew by their scent that whoever was removing the nipple clamps wasn't Barrie.

'Leave the mask on until I've gone.' It was a woman's voice. I desperately wanted to see her and considered removing the mask as soon as she'd untied my wrists, but I knew she would tell him. If I failed the lesson, I might never see him again.

When I heard the door shut, I took off the mask and looked out of the window. I saw a small dark-haired woman getting into the back of a sedan. She looked up and wagged a finger towards the window. After she drove away, I applied lotion to my nipples and took a bath. My body was stiff from lying in the same position for so long. It was almost lunchtime. I went to make myself some food and found a list of typed instructions on the table.

I'd already broken one of the rules he'd set for me by dressing. He wanted me to remain naked while he was away, except when I went for the dress fitting. He'd booked a car to collect me the following morning. I was to call no one and keep his phone next to me at all times. If it went beyond the third ring I would receive a punishment. I smiled as I read the list. How would he know if I was dressed or not? What if it was cold and I needed a sweater? I was to be in bed by ten and up at eight. I would receive a caller twice a day for an hour, one at nine and the other at four. I should be masked in the leather head covering I'd worn in Dundee and lying on the bed before they arrived. 'What the hell, Barrie,' I muttered. 'Absolutely not.'

His phone rang. 'I'm calling to check that you're OK.'

'Are you watching me right now?'

'Not right now. Why do you think that?'

'I'm a bit freaked by your list. Who'll be coming into my home?'

'I thought you trusted me. Just say if you want to stop. But if you continue, they will set up a camera, so I can watch what's happening.'

'I thought you'd already set up a camera.'

'Is that what freaked you out?'

'I have a strange woman come into my home, then I find

your instructions written and then you call me. I'm already dressed by the way. Yeah, I'm a little freaked out by everything.' I laughed. 'You being away is punishment.'

'Do you want to stop?'

'No.'

'Goody. Now I can punish you for being disobedient and cheeky to your master. Are you in the kitchen?'

'Yes.'

'Put me on speaker and take off your clothes.'

I put the phone on the counter and undressed. 'I'm naked.'

'Go to the fridge and tell me what's in there.'

'Oat milk, wine, beer, salad. I need to shop.

'What about the freezer?'

'Veggies, ice, ice cream.'

'Perfect. Take out a piece of ice, lie on the floor and hold it in your belly button, stay as still as you can.'

My pulse was racing, listening to his voice telling me what to do.

'Hold your hands above your head, close your eyes and keep your legs together. Imagine you're completely bound and unable to move. The only thing you can feel now is the ice as it melts. Try not to spill it.'

I lay on the floor listening to him tell me what we would do to me if I failed to hold the ice. I groaned as the orgasm took hold and my body shook, scattering the ice. 'Oh, Barrie,' I moaned.

'Controlling your orgasms is something you need to work on. You have an hour before the first caller. And from now on, you will refer to me as sir.'

'Really? OK.'

'OK what?'

'OK, sir.'

'Good. However, that slip means your caller will be tasked with a second punishment.'

'I thought...'

'You thought the ice was your punishment?'

'No. I mean – no, sir, of course not. Sorry.'

He ended the call without saying anything else. I mopped up the water and made some coffee, then checked the time. It was already half past three.

I put on the mask and lay on the bed. I trembled when I heard the door open. A man's voice told me to stand, and I heard the bed sheets rustling. Then a woman's voice, different from the woman this morning, told me to lay back down in the middle of the bed, face up.

I trembled when I felt gloved hands stretch my legs diagonally across the bed and secure them. They repeated the move with my arms, so I was completely constrained, with no way of easing the tension. I wondered briefly if I was ready to experience the punishment he'd planned. My nipples were clamped, and they began to use a flogger on the inside of each of my thighs. I heard Barrie's voice through a speaker: 'Do it harder.'

Just as I thought I couldn't bear it anymore, they stopped. My skin was burning. I railed against the tight bondage, aroused. I moaned.

'Control yourself.' said Barrie. 'Don't climax yet.'

I tensed the muscles in my stomach, willing myself to obey him, but I couldn't hold it.

'That's too bad,' said Barrie. 'It'll have to be the belt tonight, then.'

I assumed he meant they were going to punish me again with a strap, until I felt the metal against my labia. The belt he'd referred to would prevent me masturbating or using my vibrator.

I did as I'd been told and waited for them to leave before I removed the mask. Although I was free to move, they had left the leather cuffs on my wrists and ankles. I looked around for the camera, but I couldn't see it. I had no idea if I was being watched and recorded all the time, or just when the callers came. The intensity was heady.

Punishment indeed not to be able to climax again. I laughed out loud and thought about Mike. If he could see me now he'd realise I was as far from the prudish academic student he'd scorned as you could get. I heated some food and tried to watch a film, but I couldn't settle. I finished the wine and fell asleep on the sofa. It was almost half past eight before I woke up. Another rule broken.

I rushed into the bathroom to pee and clean my teeth. Wearing the belt all night had been frustrating. The caller would be here soon, and I hoped whoever came would remove the belt. I was certain Barrie wouldn't want me wearing it to the dress fitting.

It was a few minutes before nine when the door opened. I was masked and ready. I recognised the scent: it was the woman from yesterday morning. She removed the ankle and wrists cuffs, then the belt.

'Time to bathe,' she said guiding me off the bed, into the bathroom. 'You can remove the mask, but keep your eyes shut until I've blindfolded you.'

I allowed her to fasten the soft fabric over my eyes and stepped into the warm fragranced water. Her hands massaged my shoulders, my breasts, my arms, my belly and my thighs.

'Lean forward so I can finish your back, then I'll wash your hair.' Her voice was soft.

I liked being nurtured and cared for while she massaged my scalp.

'We don't have much time. The car will be here soon, and you should eat before you dress.'

'Are you coming with me?'

'No.'

I was curious about her role. 'Can I ask you something?' I said when she'd finished blow-drying my hair.

'No,' she said sharply. 'I will make you food and feed you so you don't mess up your face. Eating with a blindfold or a mask takes practice, until they teach you…' Her voice trailed off. 'Come.'

Even though I knew the layout of the flat, I was disoriented, just as I had been in my consulting room when Barrie had covered my eyes with his tie and told me to find the chair. The memory roused me; my nipples hardened.

I heard the swish of a whip and the sting against my naked butt. 'Do you need to wear the belt again?'

I shook my head. How was I going to control my orgasms, if every time I thought of him my body wanted to come?

She told me to kneel on the floor and used the whip. Being whipped excited me, but I stayed quiet and managed to control the orgasm.

'OK, stand. I'll dress you.'

I knew that whatever she was dressing me in wasn't from my wardrobe. The skirt moulded to my figure like a second skin. A fitted top over a strapless bra, zipped from the back. She clipped a belt around my waist and told me to sit while she helped me into shoes.

'They're six-inch-high stilettos, so walk carefully. I'm leaving now. As soon as the door closes you may remove the blindfold. Don't look out of the window again. Leave the flat when your phone beeps. The driver is will take you to the fitting and bring you straight home. You don't need a bag, but you will need your key.' And without another word, she was gone.

I looked in the mirror and hardly recognised myself. My hair was full, my cheeks rouged, and I was wearing a shade of pink lipstick I would never have picked out, but it suited me. The clothing gave me a look of retro Paris chic.

The fitting itself was uneventful. A seamstress in a back street somewhere, surrounded by fabric and lace, adorned with multiple tape measures over her plain black clothing. The dress was beautiful. Sage green bias-cut satin with a built-in bra, it showed every aspect of my figure to its best advantage.

When I returned to the flat, I undressed straight away, hoping he was watching me. I lay on the bed and started to pleasure myself. I was about to come when his phone rang. I gasped. I'd left it in the kitchen. By the time I got to it, he'd rung off.

Later, when the callers came, I waited to hear his voice, but he was silent. Whoever was in the room didn't speak either. They put on the wrist and ankle cuffs and a collar and placed me on the bed, this time on my stomach. I turned my head to the side as they stretched my arms and legs and fastened me to the straps. They used two floggers against my butt, the tops of my legs, and across my back. The stings were harsh. I wasn't gagged – I could tell them to stop – but I wanted him to enjoy seeing me bearing the punishment he'd instructed them to deliver. I'd disobeyed him. I felt elated when I crawled into bed, wishing he was inside me.

It was dark when I woke up. I was starving and sore from the flogging. His phone rang; I put it on speaker.

'Good evening, sir.'

'Good evening, Willow. How's your arse?' His tone was playful.

'A little sore, if I'm honest.'

'How do you feel knowing I'd told them to do that to you?'

'I deserved it. I chose to let them continue. I hope you enjoyed watching me, sir.'

'I did. You've done well. Surpassed what I'd expected. Which means tomorrow, the day is yours – no callers, no more punishment. I'll see you in the evening.'

'Thank you, sir, if you're sure I have done as you wished.' I was surprised by how naturally the humility tripped off my tongue. It didn't feel like I was playing a role anymore; I was enjoying our partnership and the experiences he offered me.

He took me to bed as soon as he arrived home.

'What is it?' He looked at me softly as I purred against him.

'I've never felt like this before. In the past I just pretended to enjoy sex.'

He held me tight. 'In less than two weeks, you're already a changed woman. You have more power than you had before. Can you feel it?'

'I'm not sure I completely understand how, by letting go of control, everything is bringing me so much pleasure. I know I don't want it to stop.'

'If that's true, after we return from London, you have a decision to make.'

I nodded. 'Whether I will agree to take a month out?'

'And become my partner,' he whispered, and kissed me.

Lesson Six

Barrie had booked a suite at the hotel where dinner was held. I had never heard of the charity the guests were raising money towards. Our room looked out onto Hyde Park. The autumn colours were majestic, a carpet of red and gold leaves, tempting me to run outside and lie down in them. He'd ordered lunch in the room. He didn't touch me, or ask me to touch him, until after we'd eaten.

I soon forgot about the leaves as he took me over the back of the sofa. I failed to hold the orgasm. He took a paddle from his case and spanked me. After that, we laid in each other's arms and watched a film.

I heard his alarm beep. 'Should I begin getting ready, sir?' But, just as I spoke, there was a tap on the door.

A woman dressed in a white lab coat over pale pink scrubs entered. Barrie signalled me to follow her. He watched while she bathed and massaged me, washed and styled my hair and applied my makeup. I saw her check with him throughout the treatments and styling. Finally, she helped me step into the sage green silk and fastened it over my nakedness. He handed her two boxes. The first contained earrings, dainty pearls in a flower setting to match the dress. The other box held two dark green leather cuffs and a neck collar. I looked over at Barrie as she attached a chain from either side of the collar to each of the wrist cuffs and fastened my hands behind me. She placed a pair of satin stilettos, the same colour as the dress, on the floor and steadied me while I slipped my feet into them.

Barrie nodded. 'Turn around.'

I moved carefully and slowly in a circle.

'Thank you,' he said. 'You can leave.'

The woman bowed her head towards him and left without speaking.

'Am I…' I stopped as he raised his eyebrow.

I lowered my eyes. 'Sorry, sir,' I whispered.

'You have to learn to be less familiar and honour your role. For the rest of the night, watch how the other women behave. You will not speak unless I ask you something and you will respond yes, sir, or no, sir. If anyone else speaks to you, you will do the same. Your eyes will always be lowered when you look at me or any of the other men. Do you understand?'

'Yes, sir.'

'Good.' He fastened a leash to the collar and headed towards the door. I stepped forward tentatively, unused to the height of the shoes. He pulled on the leash. 'Come, Willow,' he commanded, and I did.

I'd been concerned about how the hotel staff or other guests would react to my leash and bondage when we left the room, but I needn't have worried. No one seemed to care. By the time we got to the ballroom, I saw the other women were also leashed and wearing similar accessories. Some of them were fully masked. The circular tables were laden with silver cutlery and crystal glassware. As we made our way to our table, I watched the other women remain standing behind the men when they sat. I copied them as Barrie took his seat, then waited to see what I should do next. I didn't want to embarrass him. When all the men were seated, a bell rang, and the women sat. Barrie tugged on the leash, and I sat too.

He unfastened my hands. The chains between the collar and wrists gave me enough movement to lift my hands and reach the cutlery and glassware while the food and drinks were served. The men discussed, laughed and commented on everything from sport to politics to which punishments they preferred.

I gasped inwardly as I listened to some of the details – what they enjoyed and were hoping to watch later.

'She's ruined if she doesn't comply this time,' Barrie said.

'It was pathetic, she wasn't ready last year,' said the man sitting across the table. 'But he did brand her, so I guess we'll see.' The men laughed and raised their glasses.

I trembled. What they were discussing was far more sadistic than anything Barrie had tried with me so far. I didn't want to be publicly flogged, fucked or pierced. I certainly didn't want to be branded like a piece of cattle. I knew now wasn't the time to say I wanted to stop; I'd get through dinner and tell him I'd made a mistake when we were upstairs. This was not what I wanted for my future.

When the dinner was cleared away, the three women the men had been discussing were paraded onto the podium. Stripped of their clothing, they were each secured. One of the older men from the top table stood and made his way up to the platform. He asked each of the women for a safe word. Three other men joined him on the platform. I looked down and shuffled in my chair. Barrie leaned over and pressed his hand onto my thigh.

'These women are being honoured, Willow.'

'Yes, sir,' I whispered and looked back towards the podium. I realised none of the women were going to be brutalised, pierced or branded.

When we arrived back in our suite, Barrie removed my collar and the leash. He sat on the couch and gestured for me to join him. I lowered my eyes as he had told me to.

He tilted my face until my eyes met his. 'This is you and me now, Willow. Would you do me the honour of becoming my partner?'

I swallowed. 'Yes, but I'm confused. How do I know when it's just us, like this, and when I'm in a role?'

'As my partner, anything that happens will be because you have consented to it.'

'Those women downstairs, I thought they were going to be...' I hesitated. 'Tortured. Abused.'

He shook his head. 'I thought I'd shown you already that that's not how this works. The code is pleasure. We both honour whatever the punishment or ask is. Whatever I asked you to do would be because you have consented to it and it gives both of us pleasure.'

'What would I have to do?'

'I'd give you a really simple task. Then I would take you to a secret location for a month of immersion training. By the end of the training, if you agree, you and I would be partners. You'd promise to serve me in a public ceremony. You'd still have your flat, your business.'

I trembled while he explained what he was asking me to do. I knew that if I chose not to, I would never see him again.

'How many others would train me?'

'Maybe six, including me, and you've already met Andy.'

My eyes widened as I remembered the afternoon in the studio and the multiple orgasms I'd experienced.

He put his arms around me and led me over to the bed. 'Let's have some fun while you make up your mind.'

He told me to lay face down on the bed and raise my legs. Using cuffs, he clipped my feet and wrists together, as he had done in my flat. This time I managed the extension without moaning. He gagged me, covered my eyes and left the room. By the time he came back, I had already climaxed.

'Hmm,' he said, putting his finger inside me and feeling the warm dampness. 'You like being still, immobilized. I wonder if you can do it without being restrained.'

He removed the gag and released me.

As we travelled on the train back to Edinburgh, I fell asleep on his shoulder, his arm around me. My dreams were full of how he had used and taken me. When I woke up, my panties were soaking. I leaned over and whispered, 'I accept.'

'This is just the beginning, Willow,' he said as we left the train. 'From now on, you will know nothing but pleasure.'

Three

Middlemarch

I let out a gasp as I read the final words, *'From now on, you will know nothing but pleasure.'* Willow's decision to become Barrie's partner left me trembling.

I had never allowed myself to experience the intense sexual stimulation Barrie and Willow shared, even when Jack tried his best to love me. Despite being forty-two and married for twenty-five years, this was the first time I'd been able to relax, uninhibitedly letting my body give way to sensation, not caring what anyone else might hear or think.

Drawing my legs up under me, I hugged the pillow, moaning softly until I fell asleep.

When I woke, I saw the crescent moon peeking through the gap in the curtains. I felt as if I'd been spied on, reported, found morally wanting. I pulled the duvet over my face and tried to go back to sleep, but it was useless. I was torn between wanting to re-experience what I felt last night and guilty for the intimate pleasure I'd allowed myself to indulge in. I went down to the kitchen to make coffee.

I checked the time on the skewed clock I'd hung above the table. Jack would never have placed anything so badly, I thought, and I giggled, imagining the debacle if Jack had ever considered tying me up. He'd have made sure I was centred correctly, fussing about the materials and measuring the bed before fastening me to it. I doubted we'd have got as far as actual pleasure.

'Are your bedtimes brighter?' Heather asked when I met her for coffee at the bookshop the following weekend.

I shook my head. 'I don't think that book is for me. Thanks, though.'

'None of the stories?'

I flushed. 'I only read the first one.'

'What happened?'

I looked down, avoiding her eyes.

'I can see *something* happened. Why are you being so coy?'

'Not here,' I mouthed. I saw Audrey and Fiona from the book group approaching. I introduced Heather and explained she was hoping to join us. 'Although she may find us a bit staid,' I said.

'Oh no, I like a very broad range of fiction – and non-fiction, too, for that matter,' said Heather.

I admired her ability to nonchalantly change an awkward moment.

'Splendid,' said Audrey, chair of the book group. 'We look forward to having you.' She turned to face me. 'And, Allison, dear, it's your turn to select our next reading. Any thoughts?'

I was caught off guard. Why was *Consent* the only book title

I could think of? 'Couple of thoughts,' I said, trying to buy time. 'I'll, err, pop you an email.'

'Well don't leave it too long, dear. We're wrapping up *Middlemarch* this week. It will be nice not to have a gap, like last time.' Her smile didn't reach her eyes as the stern reminder of my earlier failure left her lips.

I nodded. 'Today, I promise.'

Heather's eyes widened as the two women left the cafe area and headed towards the well-stocked shelves of new and second hand books. 'I see what you mean. Were they Jack's friends before you met them?'

'Kind of. He played golf with some of their husbands.'

'So you're the youngest member?'

'No, one of the daughters and a niece come too, now, but they're both close to forty, so *you* would be the youngest.'

'Well, I'm thirty-eight, so it's all good.'

'I'm sorry about before. I felt embarrassed. I read the first story and I enjoyed it, but it's all so unfamiliar. I felt...'

'Embarrassed, ashamed, judged?'

'Guilty,' I replied.

'You know the only way to get rid of those negative feelings is to face them?'

'Easy said.'

'You talked about wanting to have an adventure, being jolted out of the greyness, to go on holiday and get a new job. Somewhere deep inside you is the ability to do all of that, but you've got to get rid of whatever critical voices you're hearing in your head. Think about *Middlemarch,* when Mrs Casaubon finally takes Mr Ladislaw as her husband. In a way, the story you read about Willow and Barrie is a modern-day version. Willow chooses to break free of the mundane and choose a man and a lifestyle not everyone will understand. But it's what she wants.'

I'd just taken a mouthful of coffee, and spluttered it everywhere when Heather made the comparison 'The Lesson Maker' and *Middlemarch*. I imagined Audrey's face if I offered the comparison at the next book group.

'Well if we're comparing the stories to classics, it would be churlish not to continue.' I laughed.

Heather winked. 'Good for you. But, remember, not everything works for everyone. Oh, and by the way, the colour you're wearing today – it really suits you.'

I walked home feeling more positive than I had in a long time. Heather's comments were well observed. She hadn't known me long, but already she'd shown me life had possibilities. I hunted out a Nina Simone collection that I'd downloaded and played 'Feeling Good'. When the song finished, I fetched my Kindle from the bedroom. Disobeying my own rules about drinking alone, I opened a bottle of wine, then settled on the couch to read the next story.

Four

Tie Me Up, Tie Me Down

Endings

I re-read the letter from Donald Winnicott, Esq. I was now the legal owner of the Chetan Bhavan estate. Three months ago, I'd been convinced the first missive from Winnicott and Sutherland Solicitors was some sort of scam and binned it. When a second letter arrived, my boyfriend Chris checked them out. They were legit, and so was my unexpected inheritance. A rambling Victorian house and grounds in West Riverhoe, Essex.

I never met my grandparents on Dad's side. They'd broken all contact with him after he married Mum. Why they had chosen to make a child they never bothered with while they were alive their heir was a puzzle. I knew there were cousins and other grandchildren in India. Surely they had a claim more worthy than mine.

I told Chris my plans to travel to Essex and view the place for myself the following day.

'I'm coming too, obviously,' Chris said. He pouted when I shook my head.

'I need to go alone for the first time. It's where my father was born.'

I already knew Chris wanted me to sell the estate and buy something with him in town. He'd been suggesting we move in together for a while, but I was reluctant. I liked my own space, even though we spent most nights together. He was very persuasive when he set his mind on something. I'd even stopped going out with friends co-workers to please him.

He slipped his hands under my camisole and cupped my breasts. 'Say I can come. You know you'll need my advice.'

'I…'

'Later,' he said, as his hands pushed down my pyjama shorts. He swung me around and knelt me on the bed, pinching my nipples. 'Just a quickie little, slave.'

I was wet, as he knew I would be, but he was finished before I had a chance to orgasm. He withdrew and slapped my butt.

'Good girl. That's sorted then, I'll come with you to see the house. We could take that little bag of tricks I bought for you. I can't wait to try them out – they'll be fun in the countryside.' He pulled on my ponytail, so my face turned to his. 'And keep thinking about how you'll pleasure me later, while you're planning to save the world with your hippy colleagues.'

As soon as he left the flat, I lay down on the bed and studied the picture of the two of us on the bedside table. Looks-wise and professionally, we were opposites. He was athletic, a blue-eyed blonde, stereotypical of his Californian roots. I'd inherited a combination of my English mother and Indian father's features, with black hair, light brown skin, and grey blue almond shaped eyes. He worked in the city, and I worked for an environmental charity.

'What do you see in us?' I said aloud to the photograph. We'd been together for eighteen months. He was my first steady boyfriend since university. When my parents died in a road accident, none of the other students had seemed able to understand or cope with my grief. Eventually I avoided socialising.

Chris was spontaneous and exciting; I was surprised he'd been interested in a quiet girl like me. I'd soon grown to realise, he was more than a little selfish. This morning's *quickie* and the gifts he bought me – lingerie and sex toys, ignoring my hints for perfume or a spa treat – were prime examples. I was going to be twenty-five in a week. To celebrate, he'd booked a party weekend in Ibiza after I told I'd wanted to go to Scotland.

I shook myself out of the doldrums, chose a bright yellow sundress, fixed my hair, and made my way over to the charity.

That night, Chris wanted to try out the *gifts* he'd bought for me. I agreed to wear the tight black pleather one piece, cut to expose my butt and breasts, but I refused the gag. He played with the dildo, then teased my mouth with his cock before he bent me over the bed and fucked me.

'Come on, Amirah, I'm working hard, here,' he grunted.

I closed my eyes and tried to get into the game he wanted me to play. I wasn't feeling it. I wriggled and writhed my hips, pretending to climax so he'd come.

'You sexy whore,' he said when he was satisfied. 'Tell me how you love being my sex slave.'

And, in that moment, as if someone had flicked a switch,

whatever passion or attraction I'd once felt for him had dissipated. There was no way in the world he was coming with me tomorrow. I moved against him, to get up, but he pushed me down.

'Oh no, I'm not finished yet.' He picked up a strap.

'Yeah, but I am, Chris,' I said. I pulled at the one piece and started to wriggle out of the costume. 'I don't want to play anymore.'

'What's the matter with you?'

'There's nothing the matter with me, except putting up with this for too long. I'm going on, moving on.'

He shrugged and opened his hands, as if he didn't understand what I was telling him. He stared at me without speaking. Waiting for me to finish, which was unusual.

'We're through, Chris. Our relationship is over,' I said, surprising myself by the clarity of the statement.

He frowned. His eyes cold, he raised his hand as if he were going to hit me.

When I put my hands up to protect my face, he stopped himself.

'What the hell! Why? When I do all this for you. To please you. Who else would bother with a scrawny little mouse like you?'

But the verbal punch missed. I stood straighter, legs apart, my inner warrior woken. 'You do all this for yourself. You never ask me what I want, or listen when I tell you.'

'You said you enjoyed games,' he snapped. 'You were the one who asked me to tie you up, remember? You said you liked it.'

'I did, I do, but… Oh, I don't know. Just not this.' I pointed to the dildo and costume. 'If you take what you need for tonight, I'll send the rest of your stuff over tomorrow.'

'Aren't they environmentally friendly enough for you? I suppose ropes and sacks and being spanked over a country fence would turn you on more.'

I shrugged. I didn't realise it but Chris had, unknowingly, predicted my future.

My heart was racing while he slammed doors and made a meal of organising his departure. As soon as he left, I slid against the back of the door, sighing with relief. I packed up the sex toys, detritus and clothing he'd left and organised a courier to deliver the bag to his office the following morning.

Beginnings

I was awake early and in plenty of time for the train from Liverpool Street Station. My environmental consciousness prickled while I signed papers for a car rental in Colchester. West Riverhoe wasn't far but, according to Google, there were only two buses a day.

I didn't know Essex well. Chris had taken me to a party on Mersea Island when we first met, but we'd travelled at night, and I didn't remember much about it. I turned off the A-road and drove parallel alongside the River Colne. The countryside was flat, pretty and charming. I wondered why my grandparents had chosen to settle here. Dad told me he was bullied at school and the locals hadn't been welcoming towards his parents.

The GPS announced that my location was on the left. Brambles, weeds and tall wild grasses grew untamed along the gravel driveway. The remains of a crumbling brick wall edged either side of the property. Buddleia and dandelions had self-seeded along the drive, their purple and rich yellow flowers defiant of order, attracting butterflies and bees. I parked behind a black convertible which I assumed belonged to the solicitor's junior, who was bringing documents and showing me the property.

The house showed signs of obvious distress, its former grandness no longer imposing. The windows were dull and grey with dirt. Ivy and old roses covered some of the brickwork, and the exposed bricks had lost much of their pointing.

A man in his early thirties wearing a grey suit, pink shirt and dark blue tie came through the front door of the house and strode towards me with his hand out.

'Jonathan Winnicott. Pleasure to meet you, Miss Hassan.'

'Amirah, please. I wasn't expecting one of the partners. Thank you for coming.'

He waved his hands. 'No, no – my father is the partner, I'm a mere junior.' His voice betrayed a public-school education. His nut-brown eyes were warm and friendly when he grasped my right hand in a firm handshake.

The electron charge buzzed through me as soon as he took my hand. I flushed, then swallowed. His smile suggested that the momentary frisson had surprised and pleased him. I pointed to the house. 'Shall we take a look inside?'

He nodded and led the way. 'This is the kitchen. If you're planning to live here, you'll need a lot of things done to make it safe. The electricity needs upgrading and what does work – well, frankly it's a hazard. There is water.' He turned on the tap and some unappealing brown sludge trickled out of the rusty tap. 'Obviously it needs to be run to clear.' He twitched his mouth and wrinkled his nose.

'Yeah, I get it. But it seems like a good house. Solid, I mean.'

'It's well built. Look, here are the original plans for it and the additional work your grandparents had done. The architect and the builder were well known in these parts. Lots of history. There's a local society, if you're interested.'

I looked at the documents laid out on an old pine table in the middle of the kitchen. The older plans were yellow with age, but still readable. There was a crisp white document with my name on it as the new legitimate holder of the deeds.

Apart from the kitchen, there was a dining room, parlour, cloakroom, study and an orangery. According to the valuation report, and what each room was used for, my grandmother had nurtured exotic spices and fruits in there. Upstairs were four good-sized bedrooms and a bathroom.

'There's a developer who's expressed interest, if you're planning to sell. This is a substantial size estate, and very commutable for London.'

'Thanks, but I won't be selling. Especially not to a developer. But how I'll raise enough money to make it habitable is another question.'

Jonathan nodded. 'Let me know how I can help. We've got lots of reliable local connections – joiners, electricians, plumbers.'

'Thanks. I'm going to take a look round at the outbuildings. You don't need to stay – I'm sure you've got things to do. I'm staying overnight at The Fisherman's in the village. Do you know it? Is it OK?'

'Good food, and there'll be live music later. A folk group, not that that's everyone's cup of tea.' He looked down, as if he'd betrayed a guilty secret.

Impulsively, I invited him to join me. 'Bring your, err…' I looked at his hand. He wasn't wearing a wedding ring.

'I don't have a girlfriend. Actually, I checked out of the office for most of the day, so I could show you the area. Work's pretty quiet at the moment. Lots of clients on holiday.'

'Thank you, that's kind,' I said, 'How about I check in at The Fisherman's, then you take me on that tour.'

When he picked me up from the pub and opened the door to the Audi, I noticed a tripod and two camera bags on the back seat. 'You're a photographer, or is that just for work?'

'No, I take pictures, mostly wildlife. It's what I wanted to do – professionally, I mean. But Dad had his heart set on me carrying on with the firm. He took it over from his father.'

'And the other partner?'

'Jeremy. But his daughter Dale will officially become partner next year. She's great. Her grandfather was in partnership with my grandfather. When her father took it over from him, her mother left and raised Dale in Boston. The American one, not Lincolnshire. When she died, Dale came back to live with her father. He plans to retire next year. Lord, that was a bit of a potted history. Sorry.'

'It's OK,' I giggled. 'You're very open for a legal eagle.'

He shook his head. 'Don't let my father hear you say that. I'm honestly not the son he hoped for.'

'Hey, you've been great. I had a horrible time after my parents died, with the legal stuff and managing the life insurance. My parents didn't have a lot, no property or anything, but there was a bit of money in savings. I had to fire the solicitors in the end, or they'd have had all of it in fees.'

'I guess your parents didn't have a will.'

'I wasn't as naive as the insurance company or the solicitors assumed. So I did manage to hang on to some, paid off my student loans and the course fees for the MA. So now I'm qualified, debt free, but broke!'

We drove a couple of miles out of the village. Then he pulled over by the bank of the river and pointed. 'That's a bird sanctuary and the path to the river trail. It goes all the way back to Colchester, or in the other direction, down to the sea.'

'Do you tale photographs here?'

'When I'm not soliciting.' He smiled. 'The birds, the trail and the sea offer year-round opportunities. I've got some of my work in the gallery next to the pub. Tourists seem to like it.'

'I'd like to see your work. How about you show me a bit of the trail first, then we go to the gallery?'

'Do you mind if I bring this?' he asked, picking up a camera from one of the bags.

I shook my head and put my arms in the air, in an exaggerated pose.

'Do that again,' he said, 'but over there.' He helped me up onto a small mound and walked backwards, taking multiple shots of me in different poses. 'You're a natural.'

I laughed. 'A boy at Uni was studying art and design and had me pose for him. My so-called exotic features in contrast with the grim reality of an urban landscape.'

'You're certainly that. Exotic, I mean. Oh, oops, I'm so sorry. There are all sorts of non-politically correct insults in that statement. Shoot me now.'

I laughed again. 'True, but at least you're aware. Please, stop apologising.'

He helped me down from the mound. I stumbled and fell against his chest. I felt his toned body beneath the suit and raised my face upwards, towards him.

He bent down and kissed me. Pulling me into him, he ran his hands down my back. He stopped suddenly. 'I didn't…'

'I know,' I said, reassuring him. 'It's fine, I liked it.'

He kissed me again.

I melted into him, oblivious to the passing cars or walkers.

'You're the most beautiful woman I've ever met,' he whispered into my ear.

'You're pretty hot yourself,' I said. 'I wouldn't mind…' I paused, looking at him to check if I could tell what he'd say. I was revelling in the sensation of spontaneity I never experienced before. 'Maybe more, if you're up for it.'

He brushed my cheek with his lips. 'I'd like that, too, if you're sure.'

I nodded. We climbed back into the Audi and he drove us back to the pub.

The bedroom was traditionally furnished, with flowery paper, curtains and a brass bed. As soon as we were through the door, I pulled at his tie, and he shook off his jacket. He lifted me onto him. I could feel him, swollen and ready, through the fabric of his trousers. We kissed, the urgency of the sexual tension building until we were both naked. I came instantly as he bit down on my nipples, one hand under my buttocks, fingering me before he entered. He pushed harder, I came again. He turned me over, put his fingers in my mouth. I sucked on his fingers then cried out as he pushed them into my rear, preparing me. When he finally came, my back passage was full of him.

He held me, stroking my hair. Although Chris had played with me anally using the dildo, he'd never fucked me there. I was sore and uncomfortable, yet pleasured at the same time. I closed my eyes and slept.

It was dusk when I woke. He was still there, relaxed, watching me.

He stroked my cheek. 'I should have asked you, before I…'

'I would have told you if I hadn't been OK with it.'

'Do you enjoy trying different things?'

I studied his face. 'That would depend on what, when and who. I don't like playing games that I don't want to play.'

'I agree. You should never do anything you don't want to.' His eyes softened, and he drew me close into his chest. 'Let me spoil and take care of you.'

I stood in the shower while he tended to me, lathering my breasts, my underarms, massaging my scalp. He washed my waist-length hair, wrapped me in a towel and carried me to the bed. If this turned into something more than a one-night fling, I was sure I'd want to do anything for him. Chris had wanted me to behave like a sex slave, but I was never really into it. I already knew I would willingly be Jonathan's.

Proposals

Living Earth, the charity I worked for, received a grant and seed money for a pilot project. The two outbuildings and a parcel of the land that I'd inherited were a perfect fit for the sustainable small-crop experiments.

The charity was trying to promote a return to smaller farms to support local communities and ensure the growers had a reasonable living. The grant meant that I only needed to be in London two days a week, which gave me lots of time to fix the things at the house and check the work of the local trade people I hired. In just over two weeks I already had electricity, and the water was no longer brown. The bath, shower and toilet worked. I'd transformed the kitchen and one of the bedrooms into basic but habitable and usable space.

Jonathan's house, overlooking the Colne, was a welcome and clean respite from the dirt and grime. We'd met every night since I moved out of the London flat. We explored each other's kinks and fantasies and found we shared a lot in common. I told him about what had happened with Chris and why I ended it.

'You OK? You look weary,' he said after I'd been in London for a couple of days. He took my jacket and leaned down for a kiss.

'Wine?' He handed me a glass of Chablis and patted the stool in front of the kitchen bar. 'Tell me what's up while I finish prepping dinner.'

'Uh, just the loan against the house. The bank doesn't want to give me the money.'

He wrinkled his nose. 'That's nuts. You're worth a small fortune on paper.'

'Yeah, but my income – the way the charity funds work – means I'm not regarded as having permanent employment. This contract is for two years, and the other bits I do are thanks to the lottery, which runs out next April.'

'So that means what exactly?'

I shrugged. 'According to the surveyor and the architect, if I don't get the roof repaired before winter, the exposure might affect the structure of the west wall. And they've found more damp in the orangery, so my hopes of restoring it cosmetically are a non-starter.'

'Sorry, beautiful muse, that's rubbish.'

'Muse?'

'Would you prefer what your ex called you?'

I laughed. 'In his dreams. No, I like muse, if that's what I am.'

He put down the pan and came over to kiss me. 'I have something to show you. A proposal I've sent to a publisher. After what you've just told me, tonight seems like the right time to talk to you about it. Stay there.'

I tingled excitedly and did as he asked.

He came back with his camera, a book, and a folder. 'Don't pose, just try to ignore me,' he said as he walked around, taking shots of me on the stool from above, from the side and from the floor. 'You're so easy to photograph. I'll show you the proposal after we eat.'

It was warm enough to eat al fresco. His patio was small but private. He'd built a gazebo to hold a hot tub at one end and planted vines, scented jasmine and wisteria at the other. The plants, trained up over a trellis, created a fragrant canopy above our heads. I leaned onto his shoulder, full and content, and he began massaging my breasts.

'Continue doing that and I'll be on the floor begging you to fuck me,' I said, feeling the tension from London leaving my body.

'I like it when you beg,' he said. He untied the back of my dress, slipped it down over my breasts, and then guided me onto my knees until I was facing him. I opened my lips and took him into my mouth. He sat forward, grabbed my hair, and moved my head in rhythm while my tongue pleasured him. He threw his own head back, sighing as he filled my mouth.

I stayed still, kneeling in front of him, naked from the waist up.

He picked up his wine glass. 'How was dessert?'

I smiled. 'Delicious.'

'My turn to pleasure you with a special treat,' he said, tracing my nipples with the base of the wine glass.

'What about the proposal?'

'I'd like to photograph you naked,' he said.

I trusted him, but I was a realist. I knew intimate photographs could ruin the life of an ex-lover. Many women, who'd been publicly exposed and trashed online, had once trusted those same men with a camera. 'I can't, Jonathan, I'm sorry.'

'Let me show you – explain it better. Come with me.'

I pulled up my dress and followed him inside. He passed me the book he'd brought in earlier. 'Just look through it. Tell me what you think.'

He sat next to me while I turned the pages. It was an old book with black and white photographs of a woman doing housework. She was partially naked. In some of the pictures, she was physically tied to the task. The interior settings and the woman's hair and makeup looked to be from the 1950's. The images were striking, an artistic interpretation of domesticity and the role of women.

'Where did you get this?'

'From a rummage sale a few years ago. I thought I'd like to create something similar, except outside, in nature. I have a publisher interested. Well, an offer actually. This is the proposal.' He took some paper out of the folder.

The cover of the proposal had the picture of me standing on the mound in front of the river.

'This is from the day we first met?'

'Yeah, but you're dressed in that one.'

I laughed and gave him a playful slap. 'You want me to take

my clothes off outside where everyone can see me?'

He inclined his head and rested his hand on mine. 'It could be fun, and you never know, the advance and royalties could help towards the house repairs. This is what they're offering upfront.'

I raised my eyebrows when he showed me the amount in the offer letter. 'This happened very quickly. I thought publishing took forever.'

'They've been interested in the concept for over two years. I just hadn't found the right model before. The publisher thinks you'd be perfect, too.'

'Right, but my reputation as an environmentalist would be… well, no one would take me seriously if I did this.'

'Why not?'

'Your title, for one thing. *Environmentally Yours*! Suggesting I'm up for sex with anyone who sees the book.'

Jonathan bit his lip. 'Sorry, I didn't mean to offend you.'

He went out to the patio.

I read the letter from the publisher again. He was right about the money: a share in that would certainly be enough to fix up the house. I went outside to join him. His profile silhouetted against the glowing orange and yellow sunset.

'Hey,' I said, placing my hand on his shoulder. He pulled me close. Neither of us spoke. For the first time since we met, there was tension between us. I wanted to fix it, but I wasn't going to agree to the book.

Agreements

'I'm sorry, Amirah. I got it wrong. Do you still want to play together off camera?' he asked, while I helped him tidy the kitchen.

'Of course,' I said, 'and I'm looking forward to my pleasure treat.' I reached up to kiss him.

He slipped off my dress. When I was naked, he carried me back out onto the patio and stood me by the trellis. 'Don't move.'

I nodded.

He pulled a length of plaited cotton rope from a box under the bench seat and placed it over my shoulders. With his face close to mine, he adjusted the rope so that both sides fell evenly to the floor. He crossed each side of the rope over my breasts, wove it across my shoulder blades and around my arms, tying them behind me. He slipped one end of the rope between my butt cheeks, fed it through my legs, and crossed both ends around my thighs, then down over my calves to my ankles, before tying them off.

The sensation of the rope against my flesh and between my legs was intense. I wanted him badly.

He placed two fingers in my mouth and his other hand under the rope. He pulled it deeper into my crack. My body trembled, uninhibited, euphoric. I climaxed.

He pulled on the rope between my legs again, until it was taut against my labia. When he saw me wince, he stroked my cheek. 'Pleasure and pain. I like how much you enjoy it. I think I'll leave you here all night,' he said, and he went inside, turning out the lights on the patio.

I moaned, then called his name. I could see him watching

me from behind the door.

'Are you asking for more attention?'

'Yes,' I gasped.

He released me from the ropes and took me upstairs. He'd already prepared the bedroom. He led me over to the bed, blindfolded me and laid me on my stomach, pulled my hands above my head and cuffed them together. He put something cold at the opening to my arse. 'Guess,' he said.

'I don't know.' He removed the item, rubbed my butt cheeks with liquid and used the flogger. It stung.

'Alcohol,' I said.

'Correct.'

He teased me with the strands of the flogger, before striking me again. My flesh smarted as he continued. I cried out, and he stopped.

'Enough?'

'Yes,' I said, then, 'No,' hungry for more intensity.

He brought the flogger down harder.

'Wait, I just want…' I broke off.

'Where do you want me?' he asked, probing me with his fingers.

'You choose,' I said. 'I'm ready everywhere.'

That night my dreams were vivid and erotic. I woke and felt him erect against me. I mounted him and we fucked as if the world were ending.

'What are you doing to me?' I asked afterwards, as he held me. 'I was practically a virgin when we met.'

He laughed. 'A virginal former sex slave who likes kink. Haha! You're probably the best fuck I've ever had.'

'Probably,' I teased. Then I sprung out of bed, over to the

window. 'It's beautiful today. Shall we play hooky on repairs and go to the beach?'

'Sure, there's plenty in the fridge for a picnic. We can bike the trail.'

We shared the shower; his hands massaged soap over my body, and he shampooed my hair the way he had the first time we were together.

While Jonathan was preparing the picnic, I flicked through the pages of the book he'd shown me. I checked the title, *The Housewife*. I looked over at Jonathan. 'What if the book title changed to *The Environmentalist*?'

He looked up and nodded. 'The publishers would have to agree, but if it means that you'll be the model, yes. Let's change it.'

Musings

The trail was busy as Jonathan and I biked out towards the beach. He'd packed us a gargantuan picnic, and his backpack was full of camera gear, some rope and a notebook.

'I'm not sure we're going to find a quiet spot today,' he said. The beach was full of families, dogs and vans selling ice creams.

'This is also a good example of rubbish and the environmental impact made by human beings. I mean, look at all that plastic waste falling out of the bin. If the publisher agrees to include environmental damage, this would be a great location.'

Jonathan laughed and took a photograph as a seagull flew down to investigate the wrappers. 'Yeah, but even if you stood naked next to that pile of rubbish, I'm not sure it would sell many books,' he chuckled.

'Ha bloody ha.'

'God, you look hot,' he said.

I was wearing a pale pink bikini top and black shorts. My hair hung over one shoulder in a high ponytail. He snapped a picture of me astride the bike, with my feet on the ground. I clenched my butt cheeks and licked my lips.

'Let's get away from all this.' He pointed to a cove further along the coast line. 'Over there should be good.'

The shell-covered beach was empty, save for a little blue dinghy. We put down towels and as I knelt to straighten out the edges of the blanket, I felt him behind me, pushing down my shorts and bikini bottom. Afterwards, when I turned over and wriggled back into my shorts, I saw someone looking in our direction from the top of the grass bank above the beach. It looked like they had binoculars.

'Shit, I think someone was watching us,' I said. I pointed, but the watcher took off.

'We don't know them and they don't know us. Don't worry about it. We won't be the first people to make out on a beach.'

'True,' I said, 'but he…'

Jonathan kissed me. 'Stop fretting.'

But I had a niggle in my stomach, and despite his reassurance, it didn't go away.

As the sun set and families left the main beach, Jonathan set up a scene to photograph me for the book. He helped me into the dinghy. I took off the bikini top. He wound some of the rope round my wrists and attached them to the cleat. I was kneeling on the seat, looking out towards the water. He released my hair and draped it over my shoulders, on either side of my breasts. The breeze blew whispers of it across my face. He took multiple shots from different angles.

'We're out of light,' he said. 'But some of these are really good.' He was standing in front of me, his cock close to my mouth, my hands still fastened to the cleat. He moved himself closer and brushed his groin against my face.

I nuzzled him. I opened my mouth, ready to take him.

'Not yet,' he said. 'I have plans for later.'

I showered and changed into a sundress, then sat on the bar-stool in the kitchen, watching him prepare our dinner. I'd just finished my cocktail when I felt his hands behind me.

Lifting me down from the stool, he ran his fingers up my thighs and slipped off my panties. Then he bent me over the stool. He lifted the skirt to my waist and wove rope around each of my legs, fastening them to those of the stool, up between my butt cheeks and across my body, along each of my arms, attaching them to my ankles on the other side of the stool. I was completely immobile, my body moulded to the design. I had no control over my openings or my exposed flesh.

He left me tied up while he ate, watching me from the table. When he finished eating, he removed the belt from his jeans, rubbed the leather over my face and across my thighs before using it.

'Again,' I begged.

'What do you say?'

'Please,' I said, and I gasped as the leather slapped against my flesh. He continued until I roared my climax.

'Mmmn, that's one pink bum,' he said, planting a kiss on my butt cheek. 'Now you can have your dinner.'

'Do you mind if we play hooky again?' he asked. It was Sunday morning. 'I want to try out another photograph after we've had breakfast. I'm thinking the more I send to the publisher, the happier they may be to approve the suggested changes, which means you get money quicker.'

'Sure. I was going to call the contractor anyway, to let them know I may have to delay some things.'

'Give it a few days before you call. I could probably help out if we know the advance is coming.'

'I couldn't ask you to do that.'

'You didn't. I offered.'

I kissed him.

'Not now – to work. Pleasure will come later. I promise.' He winked and headed into the shower. 'No masturbating for you,' he commanded from the bathroom door when he saw me lie back on the bed. 'Get in here and get washed with me.' He threw a satin robe over to the bed.. 'You can wear this for breakfast.'

While we ate he asked me about the growing cycle of vegetables 'What's the environmental impact of eating the same things all year round?'

'Big question. How long have you got?'

'OK, simplify it. What's in season now, locally?'

I listed all the fruits and vegetables, and he wrote them in his notebook.

'The other night, you didn't know what this was,' he said, holding up a grape.

I smiled. 'Are you going to tell me what else you used?'

'No, best not tell you everything. You like it more when you don't know what's happening. The way your body responds is amazing.'

He held out the grape and pushed it between my lips. 'Are you ready? I'm going to blindfold you for this setup.' He held up a sage-green satin scarf.

I trembled when he placed the fabric across my eyes, tying it tightly behind my head. He removed the robe and told me to put my hands together as if I were praying. He wound satin around my wrists and bound them together. Then, guiding me from the chair, he led me outside. As we left the patio, my feet became soaked with dew from the grass. 'I'll help you kneel,' he said when we stopped. 'Remain still once I've positioned you.'

He lowered me until my knees touched the grass.

'Raise your hands up in front of your face.'

I brought my hands up and heard the shutter of the camera.

'A little higher, and bow your head.'

I was in a prayerful pose. I wondered to whom or to what I was supposed to be praying. Environmental issues are caused by humanity, not deities, which I didn't believe in.

'Bend right down, stretch out on the grass in front of you, and go as low as you can with your hips raised up while you stretch.'

I thought of the cat stretch yoga pose I used to do and tried it.

'That's really good. Now stay there – I'm going to dress it up a bit.'

I shivered when I felt something cold placed on my back, then what felt like an arranged pattern of different textures, some sticky, layered across my flesh. The camera shutter snapped shot after shot.

'We agreed…' But the words stayed in my throat when his hands began to massage my butt. He turned me over, my hands above my head. Licking my stomach and breasts, then moving down to my clitoris, he used his tongue and fingers until I orgasmed.

'I was trying to stay professional, but you're far too sexy to resist,' he said, removing the blindfold and releasing my hands.

'Well, this book isn't going to be finished quickly if we keep stopping for your needs,' I teased him. 'Was any of it of any use?'

'Yeah, before my dick insisted on joining the party,' he chortled.

I laughed. 'Imagine! And what was on my back?'

'Ah, all the things that don't grow here, or are out of season. You were a fruit salad of environmental no-nos.'

'And I was praying to what?'

He pointed. 'To the good old apple tree, of course.'

We cleaned up, dressed, and watched as the late August weather turned to rain. I made a face at the gathering storm. Jonathan said, 'Seems like a good afternoon to stay cosy indoors, edit photographs and amend the proposal.'

Disagreements

He'd been right; sending the publisher his photographs, along with my writing, helped show how the environmental information enhanced the original proposal. Jonathan had asked Dale to review the contracts. As soon as they were signed they issued the advance. Jonathan and I celebrated and the contractors got to work on my house.

And then came trouble.

I was halfway up a ladder, painting the ceiling in the cloakroom, when Jonathan barged into the hallway shouting for me.

'I thought you said you'd never posed for anyone naked

before.' His face was red, eyes darting, waiting for my reaction.

Two of the workmen fixing new wood around the door paused, exchanging glances with each other, their eyes bulging.

'What the hell?' I pointed to the kitchen. 'Let's talk there. What's all this about? And please keep your voice down.' I avoided looking at the two workmen and closed the door to the kitchen.

'How do you explain these?' He thrust two sheets of paper at me. An email, with three photographs of me tied to a bed. I was partially naked and blindfolded.

'Oh God, that's my rental flat in London. I would have been with Chris! I don't know how or when he took them. I certainly didn't give him permission. I wouldn't have.' I broke off to read the email and slumped as I took it in. 'He's trying to blackmail me?' I choked.

'Yeah, my innocent environmental model who I persuaded the publisher to trust now looks like a cheap porn star for home movies.'

'What, not just photographs? There's film?'

'He claims he has images of you doing all sorts. He didn't send any clips, but I don't think he's lying.'

I covered my eyes and turned away, desperate to stop the torrent of tears. I needed Jonathan to tell me it would be alright, that he understood I hadn't had anything wrong, but he said nothing. I breathed deeply and re-read the email. 'What's this about an intention? He claims he had an interest in the property I own. That I acted to deny him his rights? He doesn't have any interest in the house, and he didn't loan me any money.'

Jonathan shrugged. 'It's a little unsound, but legally, if he can prove he loaned you money to put into the property and that you had promised him he would share in the property as your future husband, a clever lawyer could argue it. They're probably looking for an out-of-court settlement. It would be pretty risky to take it before a judge.'

I swallowed, feeling hot and cold at once. I held onto the table, then flopped into a chair and leaned forward. I felt faint.

Jonathan poured a glass of water and bent down in front of me. 'Focus on me. Count slowly: one, two, three, deep breath… and again, one, two, three…'

I followed his instructions and sipped the water slowly. 'What should I do?' My voice was thin. I felt helpless and stupid.

'You need to call his bluff. He doesn't know anything about the book, which is good. The last thing we need is for the publishers to find out, or for these to go viral online. How does he know about me, where I work?'

'I thought the first letter from your father was a scam, to be honest. Chris checked you out and confirmed your firm was legit. I don't know why he emailed you and not your father. Although I'm really glad *he* didn't see those awful pictures of me.'

'You need to show all of this to Dale. I'm too involved to advise you properly, and I daren't respond. Conflict of interest and all that.'

'No, I couldn't. Dale would despise me.'

'Dale would see this for what it is. Look how helpful she was over the contract with the publishers, and introducing us to her agent friend.' His phone pinged. 'Fuck,' he said, staring at the screen.

He handed me the phone. It was another email and two more photographs. This time Jonathan was featured, shagging me on the beach.

'So he's doing this because he's jealous!' I remembered the niggling feeling I'd had that afternoon. 'He wants a hundred thousand to stay quiet.'

'He won't stop with that. Pay him anything and he'll bleed you forever. But we do need to stop the photographs from going online. What he's threatening to do falls under revenge porn, and that's illegal. Dale can apply to the court for an injunction. You need to talk to her today.'

I clenched my jaw and nodded, then hit the table with my fist. 'Damn Chris,' I shouted.

Dale was everything Jonathan promised. Unperturbed by the pictures, she leapt into action, professionalism personified. By the end of the day, she'd issued an emergency notice alerting Chris to the injunction, which prevented him from publishing the photographs, and a letter threatening legal action against him if he didn't comply. Dale explained to me that his claim against the property was more complex than stopping him publishing the photographs.

'He doesn't seem to have sought legitimate legal advice. I'm guessing he cobbled this claim together from online sources, and he's right to a point, but where's his evidence about the loan? Were you officially engaged?'

'No. He was pushing me to move in with him. After he found out about the inheritance, he wanted me to buy a place with him, using money from selling the estate. I didn't want to, but I found it difficult to say no. That's why I needed to see the place without him. I never imagined he'd stoop to stalking when I broke up with him.'

'So could we use coercive control as an argument?'

I nodded. 'I should have ended things between us a long time ago. It sounds stupid now, but I didn't want to be on my own. Whenever I tried to end things, he always apologised and persuaded me we were good for each other, that no one else would...'

'But you did cnd it.'

'Yeah, after he made me dress up in an outfit he'd bought. The way he used me... something snapped. It was right before I met Jonathan.'

'I doubt that time he photographed you two on the beach was a chance encounter. I imagine he'd been spying on you for a while. The way he writes has traits of obsession.'

'Chris knew where to find me because he saw the letters about the property and he has friends close by, in West Mersea.' I shuddered. Chris had been the only person in my life after uni. Whenever I thought I was making a friend, he found fault with them. Even where I worked – my colleagues had become an issue. I knew that if I continued with the relationship, he would have persuaded me to sell the house. These photographs showed me just how badly things could have turned out. Thanks, Dale. I feel better for telling you everything. Although I'm really embarrassed that you now know so much about me.'

She leaned over her desk, resting on her elbows, palms upward, open. 'I've seen it first-hand, Amirah. I know what abuse does to a woman, before she even realises what's happening to her. I'm glad I could help, and I'm glad that you dumped him. But be on your guard. You *and* Jonathan.'

I had to travel back to London the following week. There'd been no more emails from Chris, and he hadn't responded to Dale's letter. Jonathan offered to come with me, but I persuaded him that I was feeling better. Then, a few minutes after I'd arrived at work, a hand-delivered envelope came for me by courier. There was no way of knowing Chris had sent the thumb drive until I inserted it into my laptop.

I froze, revolted as the footage played out on the screen. Chris didn't appear, other than his hand spanking me or penetrating me with different sex toys. It looked like I was a willing participant in the film. There were shots of me looking towards the camera, wearing a gag or licking my lips. He must have hidden a camera behind my dresser, and on the shelf next to the bed. I didn't remember most of what I saw him doing to me. There was denigration I would never have agreed to. I called Jonathan.

Jonathan sighed heavily into the phone. 'Did you and he do drugs together?'

'No, but... we drank, and a couple of times I do remember passing out.'

'He drugged you. That's how he posed you and got the close-ups. You would have had no idea what was happening. You need to go to the police. Check with Dale, but I'm quite sure that will be her advice.'

'But the injunction...'

'He's showing you his hand, but there'll be more. He wants to frighten you. This isn't just about making you agree to give him money. He wants to humiliate you and show you he's in control. You have to stand up to him.'

Settlements

Three weeks later, Chris's behaviour brought the police to my door. He'd been arrested and charged with molestation, sexual assault, possession of class-A drugs and damage to property. The police had found pornographic material of me and a number of other women when they searched his flat. Jonathan and I decided we had no choice but to come clean with the publishers.

'It's all good,' Dale told us after she met with them.

'But what if someone leaks any of the material? I don't want any of that to be seen by anyone, ever. They're disgusting.'

'Chris is pleading guilty, and the photographs of you aren't part of the trial. They won't be used at court. The injunction was agreed. You also have the right to claim compensation from Chris.' Dale's voice was calm, steady, reassuring.

'I don't want his money,' I snapped.

'Then give it to someone or something that you care about,' Dale said, shaking a finger at me. 'He's a worthless, abusive shit and deserves to pay.'

Jonathan laughed. 'That's your professional legal description, I'm assuming.'

'You'd better believe it.' Dale's American drawl exaggerated the words, making them more poignant.

I remembered what she'd said to me when I first discussed what had happened between me and Chris. She, too, had had first-hand experience. It wasn't the right time to ask her about it, but I hoped she would be able to tell me one day, if she wanted to. I hoped we would become friends.

'So we're alright to continue with the book?' Jonathan asked.

'Yes. What's the plan, now that this is all settled?'

I looked over at Jonathan. His eyes were sparkling.

'Oh, we don't tell Muse,' he said. 'She's a better model when things are spontaneous.'

Jonathan was attentive, tender and gentle when he loved me, since I'd received the footage from Chris.

'You tell me when you're ready for more than this,' he said after we made love. 'And if that's never, that's fine too.'

'Thanks for being so patient, caring. I love what we've discovered about each other, and the way we play together. If I'm still wobbly by the weekend, not up to modelling, I'll let you know.' But as the days rolled by, I felt emotionally stronger; I was the one who instigated the game on Friday evening.

Waiting for him to finish in the bathroom, I put on a white silk bra, suspender belt, laced briefs and stockings. I laid across the bed with a silk mask covering my eyes. Legs open, arms above me in a diagonal pose.

I heard him grunt with approval when he returned. Without speaking, he fastened my wrists and ankles to the bed, tightening the mask. I breathed in deeply when I heard him leave the room. The electric tension building, taking me towards a crescendo of sexual pleasure. By the time he came back, I was ready to climax.

He ran something soft and feathery over my face, then along my entire body. He followed that with something sharp and pointy. I tensed as I heard the seam of my white lace briefs rip. He removed them, placed something cold inside me, then dropped warm liquid into my belly button and rubbed it between my breasts. He traced my lips with ice and pushed it into my mouth. He awakened every part of me as his tongue licked and kissed my torso, my legs and my feet. Moving up my body, I felt his testes against my mouth, I lifted my head, trying to catch him with my tongue. Then, loosening my wrists and ankles, he pulled me up to kneel and filled me until we both climaxed.

He slapped my butt playfully. 'It seems like you're feeling better!'

'Oh, I think so,' I mumbled, exhausted. 'Thank you.'

'Happy to oblige, Muse,' he laughed.

I snuggled against him and stared at the Swiss Army knife lying next to the bed. 'Yikes, I'm glad you stopped at the panties. This is my favourite bra.'

'Well, that bra had better watch out,' he chortled wickedly.

As we drove out to Mersea Island to the sound of Santana's *Abraxas*, the roof of the Audi cabriolet down, I leaned back, satisfied. I loved how perfectly we read each other. The mutual trust, both in the bedroom and while we were working together.

When Jonathan originally proposed the book, he'd envisaged a naked model in natural surroundings. The model in the original book had been bound to her household chores. When I suggested including examples of the harm human beings cause to the environment, he suggested having me tied or bound in some way to signify wilful blindness or an unwillingness to change. The photographs he'd developed of me so far had done exactly that.

Unlike the experience I'd had with Chris, who'd taken advantage of my naivety, when Jonathan tied me up I felt nothing but pleasure. I still didn't know where we were going for this shoot, but I'd noted that Jonathan packed two lengths of braided cotton rope.

'Right-ho, this is the location,' he said, pulling over. We were at an arable farm, which stretched over to the coastline and included marshes, grassland and woodland.

'I know the owner, Sam. He agreed we could photograph here. You'll like him – he's done a lot to try and restore some of the damage to the marsh, and he's expanding the woodland area.'

'Two locations in one?' I asked.

Jonathan smiled and leaned over to kiss me. 'Your writing has taken this project to a whole other level.'

We were in the middle of a kiss when a man with a ruddy face and big features shaded under a straw hat appeared by the car.

'Good to see people enjoying their work,' he said. He was a caricature of a farmer. He took one of my hands in a strong grasp between both of his. 'Welcome to the farm.'

We followed him out to the marsh. He explained how he was trying to remove the gravel and fill, which had depleted and spoiled the original water line feeding the estuary. 'If you take that path there, you'll get down to the water. When you're finished, come back up to the house. My wife Martha is preparing lunch, but just whenever you're ready. No rush.'

'This is going to be cold, I'm afraid,' said Jonathan as I followed him to the water. He pointed to a pool next to a bank of gravel. This is where they're replanting.'

'And you want me in the water?'

Nodding, Jonathan slipped the straps of my dress down my arms and turned me round. He nuzzled into my neck, fondling my breasts as the silk fabric of the sundress fell away. My nipples responded to him and being exposed to the air. He helped me to the ground.

I lay still while he measured the rope lengths evenly against my body. He fastened them together, then wove the rope up and around my legs, over my stomach, across my breasts and around my arms, which he'd stretched above my head. I groaned, enjoying the sensation of being encased in the rope, while he lifted and placed me into position. My upper torso, head and arms were on the gravel, with my lower legs and upper thighs in the water. Ripples of water passed over my pubis.

Jonathan photographed me from several different angles, mouth open, mouth closed. Eyes, open, eyes closed. Looking sad, looking defiant. By the time he was finished, I could hardly feel my legs; they were numb from the freezing water. He untied me, wrapped me in two huge bath sheets and held me against him.

'I'm sorry, that was probably too long.'

'I'm fine,' I reassured him. Then I gasped as I felt one of his hands against my butt.

'I know just what you need,' he whispered. He pulled me over his legs as if I were weightless. Raising the towel, he fingered me until I came.

The removal of woodland on many farms was a significant factor in the erosion of topsoil and degrading the quality of food grown there. I had written a five-stanza poem from the point of view of an old tree, which the publisher wanted to include in full. Jonathan's idea for this scene was to capture me as a nymph running between the trees, then as part of a tree trunk. He tied me facing the bark of one of the older oaks. I was still naked against the tree when I heard Martha and Sam calling out. They'd brought us a flask of tea and some fresh baking.

'Oops, sorry, we thought you'd like some refreshments,' Sam said.

I couldn't turn to see them, but I felt myself flushing as my butt protruded outwards from the trunk, undoubtedly pink from the spontaneous post-shoot flogging I'd begged Jonathan for.

'Yeah, we were just finishing up,' Jonathan chuckled. I felt his swollen cock against my thigh as he tried to shield me, and fasten a towel around me, while he released me from the rope.

'Well, can't wait to see the finished book,' Sam said. 'I thought it was about environmental issues.'

Martha shook her head at him.

'It is,' I said, 'with a twist. Hopefully, it will attract a broad audience.'

Sam looked at Jonathan and raised his eyebrows. 'I take my hat off to you. I always thought you were going to make a name for yourself, until you went back to work with your old man.'

Jonathan nodded. 'And I might have just trudged along with that and taken photographs for tourists, if I never met Amirah. As well as being the model, she's a writer and a scientist. Pretty smart lady.'

'I got that impression over lunch,' said Martha. She raised her cup. 'Here's to your success.'

Reviews

'It's beautiful,' I said when I finished reviewing our proof copy of *The Environmentalist.*

Jonathan tucked a stray wisp of my hair behind my ear.

'Thanks to you, it's so much more than I'd originally intended. The words, your poetry, are captivating.'

I reached for his hand and squeezed it. 'I'm nervous about the launch. So many people have said they're coming, and then the reviews…'

'Did you get any feedback from the board, now they've seen the actual book?'

'That was a bit of a blush moment, but most of the board were enthusiastic. They're hoping our supporters will buy copies and spread the word. Only a couple of snide comments, one of them made by someone that I don't have much time for, anyway.'

'Ah, the dragon lady?'

'Apparently I'm not a feminist.'

'Ha, well she'll be shocked at the copy for the publicity campaign then. *"Every inch a feminist"*!'

'I thought that was a good line when I saw they'd used that from our interview.'

We snuggled up and watched a film before heading to bed. After twenty locations, writing, editing and trying to work on the house, I was emotionally and physically exhausted. Jonathan gave me a long massage, manipulating my neck and shoulders, where I carry stress. I fell asleep before he finished massaging my feet, blissfully unaware of the oncoming storm.

Jonathan woke me with coffee and a grim look on his face.

'What's up?'

He passed me his phone. 'I'm so sorry. I've already spoken to Dale, and she's trying to find out how on earth this happened.'

I whimpered, 'No, no, no,' when I saw the image of me and a headline featured in a tabloid, two days after advance copies of the book were distributed to the press for review.

'This isn't a coincidence. The publisher is still deciding whether to postpone the launch.'

'Postpone? I should think cancelling is more accurate!' I sat on the edge of the bed.

'Dale told me they just need to get to the bottom of what's out there and how it got online.'

'You mean the photographs Chris took? And the footage?'

Jonathan nodded.

'Oh God,' I groaned. I felt sick. I started scrolling through some of the comments that had already been posted on the newspaper site.

Jonathan snatched his phone back. 'Best not to look at anything. Hateful and anonymous posts don't make sense at any time.'

I nodded miserably. The book launch had been planned for Earth Day, less than a month away. I took the coffee downstairs and went outside. The April sky reminded me of a Turner watercolour, as the sunrise offered a golden glow through the clouds. Dappled lights danced between the leaves of the laburnum, acacia and lilacs to the east side of the garden as the breeze whispered through them.

I shivered, clasping my robe around me, imagining the breeze spreading gossip about me, wandering freely, while I remained silent. Shut up by the noise of others – the derogatory, obnoxious, salacious or judgemental voices I'd already glimpsed. How many more would there be in that chorus, now? I wondered.

'It's Dale,' Jonathan said. 'She wants to speak with you.'

He handed me his phone.

'You need to get above this,' Dale said. 'The bottom line is, whoever leaked the footage and those photographs is a criminal. They've broken the law. You've not done anything wrong, and the publisher is very much on your side. They're not going to cancel the launch. In fact, they're thinking of bringing it forward, doing a pre-launch. Are you up to attending a press conference today?'

I opened my mouth, but no words came out. I handed the phone back to Jonathan and shrugged. I felt powerless, a pawn. I watched through the glass doors while Jonathan continued the conversation with Dale from the kitchen. I knew she was right, but the coarse exploitative images Chris had taken of me wouldn't stop rolling through my mind. The contrast of those against the exquisite and sensual images Jonathan and I had created together was incomparable. Yet I was being slut-shamed, thanks to my ex. As the realisation hit me, I felt anger rising inside, like a volcano. I strode into the kitchen. 'Tell her yes, whatever I need to do.'

I ran upstairs and examined the clothes I kept at Jonathan's. None of them were right.

'You OK?' Jonathan asked, wrapping his arms around me from behind.

'I need to go back to the house. I think I have what I need there. I'm just hoping I didn't donate it when I packed up the London flat.'

Gently, he turned me around to face him. 'We can fight whoever did this. Together.'

I shook my head. 'No, this is something I need to do for myself. My voice is the one that's going to be heard, not someone speaking for me.'

'Understood. I'll support you however you need me to.'

I nestled into him. We stood, holding each other as if we were rooted to the spot.

The publisher had organised the press conference and pre-launch for three o'clock. The room was already packed full when Jonathan, Dale and I arrived. A braying crowd of newspaper journalists, freelancers, a television crew, two board members from my charity and an American chat show host, among others. The great, the good and curious. The editorial team from the publishing house spoke first, then Jonathan. Finally, it was my turn.

I stood at the podium, watching the sea of faces stare at me. Holding the room with my gaze, I read one of the poems I'd written for the book. Then I asked how many of the audience had children. Nearly everyone put up their hand.

I held up the book. 'This book wasn't created for or directed at children. It is aimed at *you*, their parents.' I cast my eye in the direction of an older reporter, who'd smiled salaciously at me earlier. I pointed at him. 'You, sir – are your children anxious about the future of our planet?'

He nodded.

'And yet, wasn't it you who wrote about me for your newspaper, trying to discredit our work?' I looked over to Dale for confirmation. She gave me the thumbs up. 'Your intention was to stir interest into unlawfully leaked material that I didn't consent to taking part in, instead of focusing on this book. Our photographs show how each and every one of us contribute to the death of our planet when we don't break the ties binding us to harmful behaviours.

'I am an environmentalist. I believe with a passion that if each one of us changed even one habit, that would have a significant and positive impact to repair the damage we have all done. Our children know it. They are relying on us to behave better. And we—' I pointed to the journalist again. '—are relying on you to report facts, not spread vulgar gossip and distort the truth about who I am. Thank you.'

I nodded and sat down.

As the applause faded, the atmosphere changed from curiosity about me to curiosity about our project. None of the questions directed at me or to Jonathan focused on the photographs Chris had taken. The American chat show host organised an interview for next week's programme.

We stayed in London overnight, courtesy of the publisher, and Dale joined us for dinner.

'Cheers.' Dale clinked her glass against mine. 'I think the publisher's legal team already knows where the leak came from.'

Jonathan raised his palms upwards. 'Hallelujah, can you say?'

'Not quite yet, but anyone running that story tomorrow is likely to get slapped with legal restraints and fined big bucks. They're working on the leaks in social media, and any links to the article as well.'

The following day, most of the papers had written enthusiastic and complimentary reviews about the book, Jonathan's photographs and my writing. The tabloid whose journalist I had picked out was the only paper who continued to pursue their original storyline.

'What a numpty,' I said as Jonathan and I poured over the reviews. A few online haters had posted abuse, but thankfully, their comments were overshadowed by the abundance of positive support.

'Hopefully Dale is right about the legal stuff and the fines,' Jonathan said. 'He deserves to be professionally screwed.'

'And me?' I purred, smiling and stroking his chest. 'Do I deserve to be screwed, too?'

Promises

I sat in the orangery, admiring my handiwork. Now that the damp had been remediated, I'd planted a lemon tree, tomato plants, rosemary and chillies. I had plans to add to the crop, and I'd found some old seed packets from my grandmother. Although I knew the contents would be dust, by now, the packets gave me an idea of what else to grow and rotate throughout the seasons.

The charity project was flourishing in the outbuildings, and the repairs to the house were almost finished, apart from some of the exterior pointing covered by vegetation. I was stalling, reluctant to tear down the roses and ivy.

I picked up the picture of Jonathan and me taken just after the official launch of our book. We were already working on a second project, this time focusing on clean water and the gap between those who have access and those who don't, especially the Indigenous communities in Canada and Australia.

'Hello, Muse,' Jonathan whispered, kissing my neck. 'That's a good pic of you and me, but we deserve something a bit more special. What do you think?'

I put my head on one side. I could tell there was a plan brewing in his mind, but I couldn't fathom it. 'What are you up to?'

He smiled, then knelt on one knee and pulled out a small blue velvet box from his pocket. 'Amirah Hassan, will you marry me? Please?'

I opened my mouth. It was the last thing I'd been expecting him to say. 'Of course I will,' I gushed, and I threw my arms around his neck. 'We've never ever talked about marriage. Are you sure?'

'Silly goose, of course I'm sure. I knew I wanted to marry you from the first time I saw you.'

'But, whenever we see a wedding you…'

'Oh, that face I pull, you mean?'

I laughed, 'If one of the brides saw you, she'd think you were hexing them.'

He kissed me and led me outside. We made love to each other on the grass under a cherry tree.

'When we're married, do you still want to play?' I asked.

'Oh yes, my love. That's never going to stop, unless you want it to. Do you want it to?'

'When you came into the orangery, before you proposed, I thought you'd come up with something exciting to tease me with.'

'So my proposal and loving you just now wasn't exciting enough?' He laughed, turned me over and spanked me on the butt. I wriggled as held me over his legs and continued the spanking until he heard me breathe out and moan with pleasure.

I put my head between his legs and took him in my mouth.

'Wanton hussy,' he whispered.

Jonathan's father was the one obstacle to our future happiness. The success of the book and our new project had persuaded Jonathan to be honest about what he wanted for his future, but his father hadn't yet accepted the reality. He blamed me for Jonathan giving up his work at the firm.

'Your Dad's not going to be thrilled,' I said as we made our way over to his father's house. I moved my fingers, dancing them across my legs, enjoying watching the diamond cluster sparkle.

'Dale will run the business better than both of those men. She's already brought in new clients, and she'll easily attract good legal staff to help her. I can't stay working there just because *he* wants it.'

As it turned out, Jonathan's father had already reconsidered. His words sounded genuinely heartfelt when he told his son that supporting him to do what he loved was better for both of them. He even fetched a bottle of champagne to celebrate.

When we arrived home, Jonathan told me to wait downstairs. 'I have that surprise you were hoping for this morning,' he said. He removed the scarf from my neck and tied it over my eyes. He ran his hands across my body, feeling the shape of my breasts under the buttoned silk dress. Lifting the back of the skirt, he cupped his hands over my buttocks and pulled me into him.

I put my face upwards and felt his finger probing me. He guided me forwards, leading me across the hallway, until I heard my heels tapping against the tiled floor at the entrance of the orangery. We stopped walking.

'Raise your arms,' he said.

I heard metal clinking against the wood. He placed each of my wrists into cuffs and fastened them to either side of the door frame. His hands explored me again, unbuttoning the dress to expose my bra, stroking the silk fabric encasing my breasts, then kissing my belly. He removed the satin panties and touched my swollen clit with his tongue. I gasped while his tongue continued. He rubbed his fingers in my wetness, then opened my back passage. I trembled; I was on the verge of orgasm when he stopped. Making sure I felt the sharp point of the blade against my flesh, he cut through the straps of the bra he had previously threatened, releasing my breasts.

By the time he entered me, I was faint with ecstasy.

I climaxed twice before he released me and removed the blindfold.

I fell into his arms.

'Exciting enough?' he asked, holding me firmly against him.

I cooed, lost for words. 'When did you fix that up?' I pointed to the iron brackets and circle hoops on either side of the frame. 'And how are we going to explain them?'

'The joiner helped, and why do we need to explain them?' He smiled. 'You said this room was going to be used for growing spices. You were wondering what else it could be used for.'

'What exactly are you suggesting we expose my baby tomatoes to?'

'It's a perfect den,' he said. 'And some of the furniture I'd like to buy is very discreet.' He pointed to a catalogue on the coffee table.

'So, it's decided,' I said. 'You're moving in here after we're married?'

'If you're OK with that. Unless you'd prefer to move into mine?'

'I'd like us to be here,' I said. 'This room definitely makes a perfect den for spice and pleasure.'

I reclined along the cushions of the wicker couch. I began flicking through the kink furniture catalogue. Jonathan joined me, and we settled into an embrace, staring out at the inky black sky peppered with stars.

Five

Courage

I reached down and touched myself. I was aroused, imagining what it would be like to have the kind of relationship Amirah had found. I bit my lip, poured the remains of the wine into my glass and sighed. Pleasuring myself wasn't going to cut it – I needed the real thing.

I envied the freedom Amirah had discovered through her games with Jonathan. Her courage to end things with Chris, standing up for herself and calling out that journalist. A stark contrast to the limited life I had allowed myself.

When I'd thrown the homemade bouquet of gardenias and roses to my best friend and only bridesmaid, I was seventeen, two years younger than Dorothea when she married Mr Casaubon. Apart from sex-ed at school and a book Mum bought me when Jack and I became engaged, I hadn't really known what to expect when Jack took me to bed. It took him almost three weeks before he managed penetration without ejaculating first. The first time he entered me was painful, and I bled a lot. After that, he was scared he'd hurt me. The next few times he tried, I lay rigid and tense underneath him. I hated everything about it, even the wet stickiness that seeped out of me afterwards. He eventually gave up. We continued to share a bed, but we lived together like brother and sister. I was thirty-nine by the time I had the courage to speak to a doctor about whether I could have a baby. When the doctor spoke to Jack, Jack said he was too old, and that was that. I hadn't pushed him into it, or given myself the chance to be with someone else. Sometimes, like when we went to see *Love Actually*, I felt my body crying out to be touched, stroked, and caressed. I just didn't want to do any of that with Jack.

I searched for the dating site Heather had shown me and thought more about it. A few days later, with Heather's help, I signed up for an account and created a profile. Two hours after that, my phone began pinging with alerts and messages from the site.

I consulted with Heather, describing the messages I thought had potential, and then replied to four. After a few chats, I accepted three coffee dates and a drink at a bar in town the following weekend.

'Your photo doesn't do you justice,' said Sam, on Saturday morning. 'You're even more attractive in the flesh.'

He was supposed to have been my second date, but he'd become the first, because the other man hadn't turned up.

Sam carried two lattes over to our table and slipped onto the bench seat next to me. The proximity of his body wasn't comfortable, so I edged a little further along. He was tall, heavyset and unfit. His swollen belly protruded under his green jumper. I thought about Jonathan's lean, toned body against Amirah's flesh and giggled.

'Thanks,' I said, trying to find kind words, a way to return the compliment. Nothing came. 'And you look nothing like yours' stuck in my throat. Online, he'd presented as a rugged outdoorsy type with a mop of dirty blonde hair. The reality was a red-faced beer-drinker who ran out of breath walking across the road to the coffee shop.

I said goodbye as politely as I could and messaged Heather, confessing that I was in two minds about whether to cancel the bar date scheduled for later. When Heather replied, she persuaded me not to cancel. She was in Spain enjoying a spontaneous mini break with an Australian.

'Talk about *"Tie Me Up, Tie Me Down"*... he has all that going on and then some,' she told me, while he was taking a shower.

'Do you think he could be the one? I mean, if you both like...' I paused, not sure what they were into and not wanting to know too much detail.

'Hmm... nope, don't think so. Great cock, lots of kit and kink toys, but not much conversation, and he needs to work on his foreplay.'

I laughed. 'So much for not wanting too much information. I should have known better!'

'I'll be back late tomorrow,' she said. 'Let's catch up Monday night. Oh, and for the date later, wear that blue top or your black wraparound dress.'

She clicked off before I could reply.

Harris had already had several drinks by the time I got to the bar. He, at least, looked like his profile picture, but the smell of alcohol, a phoney transatlantic drawl and his constant reference to westerns and cowboys soon told me we didn't have anything in common.

'So, darlin',' he said loudly, after he gulped another Jack Daniels on the rocks, 'we gonna hit your place or mine?'

I was still only halfway through the glass of warm and not particularly good chardonnay he'd ordered for me before I arrived. There was no way I wanted to spend any alone time with him. The woman behind the bar caught my eye, letting me know she was watching out for me. I remembered Heather's advice, to make sure I spoke up for what I wanted and not get side-lined into pleasing other people.

'Neither, I'm afraid,' I said more confidently than I felt. I gripped the bar stool.

'Just another teasing time-waster,' said Harris, pushing his face too close to mine. He slammed the glass on the bar and staggered his way to the door.

I felt frozen to the spot and shuddered as I downed the rest of the chardonnay. I'd just slipped off the bar stool to head home when I heard a familiar voice.

'Allison?'

I turned around. It was Peter! We'd worked together for almost five years. He'd left his post at the council before Jack died.

'How nice to see you!' Then hesitated, wondering what he'd seen and heard.

'Good to see you, too. How's Jack?'

'Dead,' I said flatly.

'Oh, I'm sorry, I had no idea.'

'No, *I'm* sorry, I shouldn't have blurted it out like that. Are you visiting family?'

'Not exactly. My wife, Rachel, left me. I've just moved back.'

I sighed, reaching my arm out towards his. 'And the children?'

'Living with her, but I see them every other weekend.' He shrugged. 'It was better for them to stay at the same schools and in the same house. Do you want another?' He pointed to the wine glass I'd left on the bar.

'Not of that, thanks. It was awful. But a G&T would be lovely.'

After he'd been served, we moved away from the bar, to one of the tables.

'So, that guy who bumped into me at the door… he wasn't exactly who you expected?' Peter grinned wryly and winked.

'I don't think I have the energy to meet number four tomorrow,' I said.

'Ah, Tinder love. It's tough going, not that I've tried it myself yet. If you fancy doing something else, I was planning to take my boat out. Do you sail?'

And suddenly the dreadful evening turned into fun. Peter made me laugh, and we exchanged the woes and the upsides and the challenges of loss, living alone and daring to start again.

'I'll pick you up at nine,' he said as we left the pub and made our separate ways to the west and north sides of town.

I was about to pull down the kitchen window's blind when I saw a shooting star travelling behind the trees at the bottom of my garden. It was a magical moment. I felt as if I had finally found the path I'd been looking for. I hugged myself, then skipped up the stairs, looking forward to the next story on my Kindle.

Six

Judging Emily

The Evidence

'All rise,' announced the judicial assistant. Emily entered the courtroom, stared up at the packed gallery and breathed deeply; this case, with two of her husband's friends as defence and prosecuting council, was going to keep her on her toes.

Emily adjusted the back of her robe as she sat. Crossing her ankles, she glanced down to admire the new black patent stilettos Wills had bought for her. Her tummy fluttered as she remembered him telling her to stand naked, apart from the shoes, in front of the mirror that morning, then taking her over the chair. There'd been no time for breakfast.

Emily outlined what she would and wouldn't tolerate from the press and the gallery as she began the formal proceedings.

The prosecutor approached the jury to lay out his case.

'Mr. Daniels,' Emily said, as he paced back and forth in front of the bench, 'please remain in one position. You are making us all seasick.' The public laughter was soon silenced by Emily's glare; she banged her gavel firmly against the wood.

'I am sorry, My Lady. My feet will be firmly rooted from here on.' And he continued his speech.

Emily nodded. They had been cohorts at university. The defence council's walnut brown eyes glinted as if he were trying to convey a message. Emily caught his stare and raised her eyebrows.

'Thank goodness today's over,' said Emily, taking off her robe. 'This trial is booked for ten days, and those two mongooses flapping about are making me less than patient.'

The judicial assistant inclined her head. 'Anything else I can do for you?'

'Not right now, but thank you for keeping things on the straight and narrow, Glenda. I appreciate it.'

Glenda adjusted her bag and raised her hand in a wave. 'See you tomorrow.'

Emily opened the drawer of her desk. She poured herself a generous tot of whisky and settled to read her notes from the proceedings while she waited for Wills to pick her up. Her phone rang.

'I'm running late,' Wills said. 'I won't make it across town for ages. Can we eat at home? And I just got a text from Daniels – what on earth did you say to him?'

Emily laughed. 'He was poncing about, so I told him to stop. Court isn't a theatre, as much as he'd like it to be.'

'Once an actor, always an actor. He's never quite got over his earlier ambition.'

'Well he's not performing in *my* courtroom. OK, I'll see you at home. It'll have to be leftovers. I'm not cooking.'

'That's you on the naughty list, then. What sort of a wife are you?'

'I like being on the naughty list – or are you bored with our games?'

'Oh God,' Wills moaned into the phone. 'Stop, my cock is fit to burst.'

'Better think up a punishment, then,' she whispered before she clicked off.

She had just finished boiling the pasta when Wills came up behind her and lifted her skirt.

'Where are the fuck-me shoes?' he asked, while his hands explored her scantily clad bottom.

'This is boiling water, Wills. We don't want that cock of yours to be permanently scarred.' She laughed, bending and jiggling her arse into him.

'Daniels was right, you do need bringing down a peg or two, My Lady Judge.'

Emily turned and peered over the top of her glasses at him. 'He said that! Pour me wine, you dog. Now.'

After they had eaten and finished watching an episode from a box set, Wills stroked his wife's cheek. 'I think I'd like to…'

'Mm, me too,' said Emily, reading his thoughts. She ran upstairs to their bedroom and lay on their bed. Wills followed and undressed her. Once she was naked, he strapped her to the brass bedframe and began to play a favourite game. He teased her with a wand and described the different ways he wanted to fuck her. By the time he entered her, she was so wet she orgasmed at once.

He pumped her harder.

'I want to suck you,' she purred as the second orgasm bolted through her body.

Straddling her face with his thighs, he finished himself in her mouth.

'You're perfect, wife,' he said, combing her long, burnished-copper hair and plaiting it after they'd showered.

'And you, husband,' she said, putting her hands behind her to pull him closer. 'But those mates of yours. To be honest, I'm not sure how I'm going to survive without losing my rag at the muppets, having them both in the courtroom at the same time.'

'Yeah, too bad they're on the same trial. Could be worse – at least George isn't there.'

Emily shuddered. 'Yes, thank God! Do you remember how they used to tease me, saying I was indomitable as a barrister? I mean, it's true. I hardly ever lost a case. Now I'm a Judge, their teasing is... well, it feels...' Emily shook her head. 'Oh I don't know, ignore me. I'm just trying to do the best I can.'

'You always do, Ems. The smartest in the group and the youngest to take silk, then one of the youngest judges on the bench. Of course, because you're not a member of the quill and whip club, so you're not top of everything.'

Emily laughed. 'Oh, the hangout for men of law who pay girls to do mucky things their wives won't do. Why did you bring that place up? Don't tell me you went there with Daniels.'

'Gus was there, too.'

Gus was the defence barrister in Emily's trial.

Emily rolled her eyes. 'And you, are you planning to become a member?'

'No, I have a mucky-ducky wife who'll do anything I want.'

'So, your point is...?'

Wills shrugged. 'It was just banter. Forget it.'

'Come on. Tell me.'

'OK. Remember that night in college, after you achieved the highest marks of the cohort, *again*! We all got really drunk. The other girls left, and you danced on the table. You mocked them, because their dates had left. You said that they'd never get a woman to do what they wanted. But if they made it to silk, you would oblige. They could do anything they wanted. Then we left and went off to fuck.'

'Did I really say that?'

'Yeah. I knew you didn't mean it, but they still bring it up. They kind of took you seriously.'

'You're kidding me! It was a joke. Actually, I think I was being a bit mean.'

'Yeah, that might be the point, Ems. So I wondered – I mean, if you're OK with it – if we could expand our game. They finally get a woman, you, to do what they want, and we get to spice things up a bit.'

'Spice things up a bit? How dare you!' she screamed. She flew out of the bathroom.

Wills followed her. 'I'm sorry, Ems, I...'

'Go and get some fresh water from downstairs,' she demanded. As soon as Wills was in the hallway, she locked the bedroom door.

Moments later he was tapping urgently on the door. 'Ems, let me in, please. I'm sorry.'

'Go fuck yourself in the spare bedroom, Wills. I'm going to sleep.'

Wills's Defence

When she woke, Emily unlocked the bedroom door.

Wills arrived soon after with a tray of coffee and her favourite breakfast: fruit, French toast and maple syrup. 'I don't want to start the day in a row. I'm sorry. I'll talk to them, put a stop to the banter. I shouldn't have told you.'

Emily stifled a giggle. 'When did you and the muppets discuss it?'

'A couple of weeks ago, when we were very boozy. Daniels asked me if I'd talked to you about it when he phoned yesterday.'

'That explains why he and Gus were so weird in the court-room. They both kept staring at me as if I were supposed to know what they were thinking.' Emily slid into bed and patted the duvet. 'I'm sorry I kicked you out of our room.'

'Will you forgive me, milady?' Wills appealed to her with a doe-eyed expression from under his mop of chestnut-brown curls.

'I'll consider it.' Emily pointed to the tray. 'Now feed me, I'm starving.'

Wills obeyed and slipped the syrupy toast into Emily's mouth. After a few bites, her chin was sticky with maple syrup. Wills leaned in to lick it.

Emily giggled and put her head back. 'You like me, sticky Wills,' she said, pulling down the top of her silk chemise. Her nipples aroused, she pushed his head into her full breasts and put a hand inside the coverlet to explore her mound.

Wills kissed her breasts and pushed her flat into the bed. 'Don't come until I'm inside you,' he commanded, sliding under the coverlet to join his wife. He flipped her over and spanked her. 'That's for chucking me out the bedroom. And this,' he said, slapping her harder, 'is because you're a tease.'

Emily groaned. 'Just fuck me Wills.'

'Not yet. My Lady Judge might rule from the bench, but in bed, *I'm* in charge.' He reached over to the wall and unhooked the flogger. 'How many do you deserve?' he asked, striking her butt. 'How many until sitting in the courtroom is so painful, all you'll think about is me?'

Emily cried out, relishing the sting of the flogger against her flesh. 'Harder,' she said, as the orgasm overwhelmed her.

He pulled her into a kneeling position and pumped her until he felt her muscles contract again and they both climaxed.

'Jings, Wills, what time is it?' she asked moments later. 'Help me dress and fix this mess. I need to get to court.'

Sliding out of his embrace, she shook her hair free from the plait.

Wills ran a brush through her thick tresses and twisted them into a chignon. 'You're one feisty redhead, Ems,' he said, and planted a kiss on her shoulder.

'I'm *your* feisty redhead, Wills, don't forget that. But you know, maybe we shouldn't rule out a little spice.' She winked and bent over to put on her shoes.

'You mean... with the guys?'

'Let me think about it, but don't say anything to them yet. I'd like to have a little fun of my own in court first. Give them a good reason to think I deserve whatever they'd like to do to me.'

Wills laughed, helped her with her jacket and pulled her into him. 'I'm hard just imagining it. But you're right, you are *my* feisty redhead. It's up to you to choose whatever spice you think you're OK with.'

Emily's Rules

Emily watched Gus carefully. Even though his cross examination of the witness was on point, she still interrupted him three times. She did the same to Daniels, enjoying their growing frustration. Gus re-phrased the question. Daniels shuffled his papers, angry at the interference.

Emily didn't want to risk an appeal or a mistrial; she decided to put them both out of their misery. Just before the court was due to break for lunch, she called both barristers to the bench.

'Mr Daniels and Mr Wright, do I need to remind you again of the rule of law, and moreover, the rules of my courtroom?'

The two men shook their heads. 'No, My Lady.'

'That's better.' Emily lowered her head and leaned across the bench. 'I've had my fun. After the trial, it will be your turn, if you promise to concentrate on the case in hand,' she whispered.

The men looked at each other, then back at Emily as she raised her gavel to announce lunch.

Emily swept out of the room, followed by Glenda. She took off her shoes, sat behind her desk and pulled out her phone to text Wills. 'I've decided it's yes, but with caveats.'

'My Lady,' said Glenda, when Emily looked up. 'Can I ask you if everything is alright? We couldn't hear your instructions to council, just at the end there. What you said isn't recorded.'

Emily twitched her lips, amused by what the recorder might think if she repeated what she'd said. 'It's fine, Glenda. Daniels and the defence just needed a bit of professional encouragement. I think we'll be alright this afternoon.'

The only time she and Wills had included a third person in one of their games had been a year after they were married. Emily closed her eyes and thought about the first time they'd played a game with Rachel.

They'd been teasing each other, playing the game of 'who else would you like to fuck' in the local wine bar. Wills said he had taken a fancy to the owner. 'Rumour has it she's a swinger,' he whispered across the table.

Emily raised her eyebrows in surprise. Rachel was plump, late forties, with bottle-blonde hair, and she enjoyed flaunting her cleavage. The opposite type to Wills's usual taste.

'So what would you do if she was willing?' Emily asked.

'I'd get her to spank you while I watched, and then I'd fuck you while she watched.'

'Ha, but I bet you wouldn't ask her,' teased Emily, daring him.

'Is that a dare?'

'Sure is.'

Wills rose from the table and headed over to the bar.

She could hardly bear to look when she saw Wills lean his head close to Rachel's. Peering through half-closed eyes, she watched the exchange between her husband and the bar owner, her cheeks burning.

Rachel gave a deep-throated laugh and looked over to the table where Emily was sitting. She winked at Wills and handed him two fresh glasses of wine before moving away to serve another customer.

'She said yes, if you want to,' Wills said. 'She said she'd fancied the pants off us both since we first started coming here.'

'Wow, that's um…' Emily paused. She liked the *idea* of the scene Wills had described, but she wasn't sure she wanted the reality. 'Do you want to?'

'Only if it's what we both want. She suggested we join her

for a nightcap upstairs when the bar closes. We're not busy tomorrow, and we'd spend most of the night playing, anyway.' Wills traced her mouth with his finger.

Emily could see by the way his eyes sparkled that he was excited by the prospect. 'So, just to talk tonight, right?'

Wills shrugged. 'I guess so.'

When the other customers and staff left, Emily followed Rachel upstairs, with Wills close behind. He put his hands under her skirt as she climbed and pinched her butt.

Rachel watched them from the top of the landing. 'Let's agree to some rules before you both get carried away. Wills said this is your first time as a couple with someone else?'

Emily nodded.

'Emily, this was Wills's idea, are you OK with it?'

'I think so. What do you mean by rules?'

'You and Wills play games. He ties you up and you enjoy it. But you both know when to stop.'

'Yes. He ties me up, teases me and spanks me, and I enjoy that.'

Rachel smiled. 'And if I tied you up, do you think you'd be OK with that?'

'Yes, yes, I'm sure I will, as long as Wills is here. I'd be doing it for him as well as for me, I mean.' Emily wasn't used to being unclear in her thoughts and stumbling over her words.

'I have three rules,' said Rachel, holding up as many fingers. 'No one does anything with which they are not completely comfortable. No choking. And, finally, what happens here stays here. Do you both agree?'

'I agree,' said Wills, 'and I'd like to add that Emily has the final say. If she says stop, we stop. Whatever stage things are at.'

'Emily?'

Emily took a deep breath. Things were moving more quickly than she'd bargained for, but this setting of rules was turning her on. 'I think you've both covered everything, except...'

Wills and Rachel waited for her to continue.

'I don't want Wills to *fuck* you.'

Rachel laughed. 'Honey, that's not a problem. I don't do that unless it's a party. I'd already told Wills that wasn't part of the deal. Here, more wine.' Rachel held up a bottle of Garnacha. 'It's better than the one I served you in the bar. I'm pretty fussy. Although the wine downstairs is good, it's not *this* good.' She pointed to the wine rack in her living room. 'One day I'll have a proper cellar, but this suits me for now.'

Rachel joined Emily on the couch, and the two women clinked glasses. When Emily finished her wine, Rachel took her by the hand and led her into another room, with Wills following.

The room was sparsely furnished, and Emily gawped when she realised it had a designated purpose. There were hooks on plinths along one of the walls, straps with a swing hung from the inside of the door. Various sex toys, floggers, crops and whips were displayed on a shelving unit. In the middle of the floor was a black leather mattress in a wooden frame with hooks and straps attached to it.

Rachel guided Emily to the mattress. 'Kneel,' she said.

Emily looked at Wills, checking in with him.

He nodded.

Rachel pulled down Emily's skirt and told her to lie on the mattress. Slipping a pair of handcuffs onto Emily's wrists, she fastened her hands together, then removed her panties. 'Nice butt, Emily. It'll be perfect when it's pink. Open your legs.'

Emily obeyed.

Rachel fastened leather cuffs around Emily's ankles and fixed them diagonally to each side.

Emily heard Wills say, 'Yes.' She lifted her head to see him, but he was on the other side of her. She turned her head, but when Rachel placed a blindfold over her eyes, she realised what Wills had agreed to.

Rachel placed a wedge under hips. 'How many, Wills? What does she deserve, this wife of yours?'

'Make her arse really sting,' he said.

Emily moaned with pleasure as Rachel struck her with the flogger.

'Oh, she likes that too much,' said Rachel. 'Choose something else, Wills.'

Emily heard Wills moving things around on the shelf.

'Try this,' he said.

Emily shuddered as the crop landed on her arse. Unlike the flogger, its sharp single stroke concentrated the sting. She moaned again; she knew she wouldn't be able to hold her orgasm much longer. She needed Wills inside her. 'Please, fuck me, Wills,' she gasped.

Rachel laughed. 'What do you think, Wills, enough? Does she deserve you yet?'

'No,' said Wills. 'I want to see how long she can hold it.'

'Ooh, Emily, this man of yours – you must have been really bad to him.'

Emily's body shuddered as the climax took her. 'I need to stop,' she said.

'No problem,' said Rachel. She removed the blindfold and released Emily from the straps. 'That was brave, Emily, for your first time.'

Wills knelt beside her and stroked her hair. 'I shouldn't have…'

Emily put her hand up to stop him. 'Oh, yes you should. I was enjoying it a little *too* much. That's why I needed to stop.'

Wills frowned. 'I don't understand.'

'I do,' said Rachel.

Remembering the scene aroused her. She put her hand between her legs and rubbed herself. She imagined Wills kneeling on the floor in front of her, sucking her juice. She had just climaxed when she heard the tap on the door.

'Five minutes, My Lady.'

Emily smiled at the timing and readied herself for the afternoon session.

She glanced briefly at the notes she'd started in the book. She acknowledged her anger at Wills last night had not been because he'd suggested involving the others, but because, ever since that night with Rachel, she herself had often wanted it. She was afraid exploring sex outside of them as a couple would mean Wills would never be enough to satisfy her.

That night, Emily begged Wills to punish her for her behaviour and relished in the pleasure as he restrained and used her, making her come over and over again.

'You're sure about this, Ems? You really do want to go ahead?' Wills asked the following morning.

'Definitely,' said Emily, and hugged him.

Wills arranged to have dinner with Daniels, Gus and George that night. Emily invited Rachel for supper and told her what she and Wills had planned.

Although they had never repeated their shared experience, Rachel and Emily had become friends. Rachel understood Emily's needs and her concerns about opening up their shared love of bondage to include other people. When she and Wills moved into their newly-built executive townhouse, south of the Thames, Rachel helped them select toys, fixtures and furniture Wills could suspend or strap Emily to. Innocent-looking chests and cupboards hid a multitude of straps, whips, masks, costumes and equipment designed to discipline, punish and give pleasure. They hung a flogger above their bed, but when guests came, they claimed it was just for fun. Nothing else was on display.

Rachel smiled, but her warm brown eyes were cautious. 'Just remember that you're the one in control. You're quite capable of saying stop.'

Emily giggled. 'Yeah. And you guessed why. Wills didn't have a clue, bless him.'

Rachel nodded. 'People snigger behind my back. But they don't understand that I made a choice about the way I wanted to live my life a long time ago. You were already married to Wills when you realised one man was never going to satisfy you, despite how much you adore him.'

'If I'm honest, I think I did already know. The night when I teased his friends, when we were at college, I was hoping that something would happen before Wills and I left them.'

'You weren't ready. Too young, no experience. Most of the people I hang out with are a lot older. Which is why, if you'd like me to be involved, I'm offering to help, as a sort of supervisor.'

'What do you mean?'

'These guys have no idea what you and Wills get up to, have

they?'

'None at all. It took Wills and me a while to figure things out. I had to show him what I wanted and then let him find his own level of comfort controlling me. He didn't want to at first. Now he loves it, and not just because he knows I do.'

'Exactly. They've watched porn or seen pictures and thought they'd like to show a woman what's what. They won't realise the importance of safety, that you're consenting and that you can change that consent at any point.'

'I think they want to humiliate me, but for the wrong reasons. I'm worried about how Wills will feel afterwards.'

'You need a plan. Show me the list you made, your caveats.'

Emily handed Rachel the notebook she'd been writing in.

'You need a how, what and when. This is too abstract.'

Emily nodded. Rachel was right. She poured more wine while and Rachel made a list of suggested activities that would keep Emily safe.

'I have an idea,' said Emily, after she read through their notes. 'We could have a mock trial. You play the judge and hand out my punishment on a case-by-case basis. Wills can be the prosecutor.'

'Love it, but what about a jury?'

'Not required. I'm pleading guilty. You can sentence me as you see fit.'

Emily's trial was planned for the following Sunday. Emily and Wills moved the dining table to resemble the bench where Rachel would preside. They placed two chairs in front of the bench and a stool from the bedroom in the centre of the room.

Emily tingled as she watched Wills choose a costume for her to wear. She had swept her hair back into a long ponytail and applied a scant amount of makeup: pale shimmery lips and mascara.

'You look beautiful, Ems,' Wills said as he finished fastening the dark red silk wraparound dress. He'd also selected a thong, a black garter, natural-coloured stockings and black stilettos.

After everyone arrived and was seated, Wills instructed them in the dining room, and Emily made her appearance.

She enjoyed hearing Gus, George and Michael gasp as Rachel led her into the room on a leash with her hands cuffed behind her. Rachel handed the leash to Wills, who then strapped her to the stool.

Emily looked down and grinned when she saw Michael Daniels adjust his cock under his trousers. He wasn't going to last long if that was all it took, she thought.

Rachel was enjoying her role as Judge, using the gavel and making direct eye contact with Michael. Her cleavage spilled out of the tight black corset she wore under a diaphanous scarlet dress.

'And Mr. Daniels's complaint against Emily is?' said Rachel.

'Humiliation,' he said.

'Your claim is that the defendant humiliated you professionally. Is that correct?'

Michael nodded.

Rachel looked straight at Emily. 'How do you plead?'

'Guilty, My Lady,' replied Emily.

Rachel took out the list of punishments Emily had told her she would enjoy when they had dinner.

'Any mitigating circumstances, before I sentence?' Rachel looked at Emily again.

Emily shook her head.

'And the prosecution. What level of severity do you consider proper to punish the crime?' Rachel asked Wills.

Wills looked at Emily, then at Michael, before answering. 'Not very severe in this case, My Lady.'

Rachel beckoned Wills to approach and handed him a piece of folded paper.

Wills read the paper and handed it to Michael, who flushed while he read it.

'Next case,' Rachel said, treating the room to her deep-throated, infectious laugh.

It was George's turn. Emily hadn't seen George for at least six months. The last time he'd made a clumsy move and brushed himself against her, feeling her up during a party. Emily had put her hand over his crotch and pinched his balls hard. 'No fucking way will I ever let you touch me, George.' Wills clapped when Emily told him how she'd managed things and reassured him he didn't need to speak to George.

'And the charge is?'

'Common assault in public,' said George.

Emily raised her eyebrows.

'How do you plead?'

'Guilty,' said Emily, through gritted teeth.

'Are you seeking moderate or significant punishment?'

'Significant,' said Wills. He winked at Emily.

Emily rolled her eyes and shook her head. Wills would pay for that later.

Rachel beckoned Wills back to the bench to collect her verdict.

Emily looked at George as he unfolded what Rachel had written and shuddered at the look on his face. He was her least favourite of Wills's friends. But because he'd been there that night in college and was part of the group, Wills had persuaded her to include him.

Rachel banged the gavel against her makeshift bench. 'Final case before court closes.' Her eyes searched the room and looked at Emily as Gus came forward.

Emily nodded, realising Rachel was checking she was alright to continue.

'The charge is?'

'Broken contract, My Lady,' said Gus.

Emily put her head on one side. What did he mean? She searched back in her mind, then remembered she'd promised to help Gus prepare for an interview before she became a Judge. But she and Wills had taken off for a last-minute holiday. Although she'd sent him some notes, they weren't detailed, and Gus wasn't offered a place in the chambers. Emily snorted quietly. Was that the best he could come up with? He'd have done better using the drunken snog and fumble they'd had before she married Wills.

'How do you plead?'

Emily was tempted to mix things up a bit and plead not guilty; she was becoming bored with the game.

'Guilty,' she replied.

'And the prosecution, severity for this punishment?'

'Extremely severe, My Lady,' said Wills.

Ah, I told you about the fumble, didn't I? Emily reflected. Clever boy to suggest that none of the others know it happened.

Wills smiled at Emily as he handed the punishment Rachel had prescribed to Gus. 'Enjoy, old man,' he said, patting Gus on the shoulder.

Emily smiled, excited by Wills's obvious pleasure in what he knew Gus was going to do with her.

Rachel banged the gavel and brought the trial to a close.

'Drinks, I think,' said Wills. He beckoned to the men to leave the room. Emily was still leashed and strapped to the stool.

Rachel released her. 'You OK?'

'Oh yeah,' said Emily. 'I'm not sure Michael is going to make it through, given he almost spilled into his pants when you brought me into the room. George will no doubt relish his role, and Gus – well, let's just say I can't wait. What did you choose for each of them?'

Rachel put her finger to her lip. 'Now that would spoil the surprise,' she said.

They joined the men for drinks. Michael flushed every time Emily caught his eye. The other two were cooler, more measured. Emily knew that whatever Rachel had told each of them they were allowed to do wouldn't happen today. She was at their disposal, but she didn't know when or where. The anticipation of whatever was going to happen made her want to orgasm. As soon as everyone left, she took Wills upstairs.

Michael

The following day, when she took her seat behind the bench at court, she conducted herself outwardly with professionalism and clarity, while inwardly she was excited by the prospect that something might happen to her later. Over breakfast, she had tried to get Wills to tell her Rachel's verdicts and the punishments each of the men were going to deliver, but he refused.

'Keeping you in the dark is part of the pleasure, my love,' he told her.

She realised something had been planned as soon as she arrived home and Wills told her not to go upstairs but to remove her dress. She saw that he'd set up the bondage board in the dining area with a display of floggers and paddles. Wills had had the board made especially for her. He fastened a mask over her head then bent her over the board and strapped her hands and feet to the bottom of each side, her butt raised over the top of the curve. She couldn't see anything, but she heard him cooking.

Emily heard the back door open. Whoever had entered didn't speak.

'Go for it. Everything you need is right here,' Wills said to whoever was in the room. They didn't reply, but from the tentative first slap on her arse, Emily guessed it was Michael. He was way out of his depth, as she'd known he would be.

'Let me show you,' Wills said, and she felt the full force of a paddle. The next strike was less tentative, then another and another.

Michael was getting into his stride, but even so, she could barely feel it; feebleness wasn't doing anything for her. 'Show him again, Wills,' she said, but the spanking stopped, and she heard the backdoor close.

Wills unstrapped her, carried her up to their bedroom still masked and fucked her doggy style.

She purred when he removed the mask and snuggled her into him.

'Oh, that was pathetic,' she said later, as they shared the food he'd made. 'I mean Michael, not you.'

Wills chortled. 'Yeah, he was supposed to be inside when you came home. But he stayed outside watching. The look on his face when I put on the mask and strapped you to the board… honestly, I thought he was going to pass out.'

Emily shrugged. 'At least he can't say he wasn't given an opportunity.'

'Too bad. It'll be better next time, more fun. '

'Who?'

Wills grinned. 'Your least favourite friend.'

Emily groaned. 'Not so sure I'm looking forward to that, but hey-ho, maybe it will be alright.'

'Rachel picked a good one for George. You'll enjoy it.'

That night Emily dreamed about Michael. Wills had strapped her into the swing, and he was showing Michael how to punish and tease her. When she woke up, she made a mental note to suggest it to Wills. She liked Michael; it would be a pity if he didn't want to try again.

By the end of Wednesday, Emily's patience was thin. Michael fumbled and stumbled his way through the proceedings. Emily had shown him as much grace as she could, but she couldn't let his mistakes ruin the chances of a fair trial. She called him to her chambers for an unofficial meeting after court had adjourned for the day.

'You need to get your head back in the game,' she said as he sat opposite her. 'You're a good barrister. Behave like one.'

'My head is all over the place, Emily. Every time I look at you, all I see is... I didn't know anyone would like that. None of the women I've had a relationship with wanted me to do that to them.' He shrugged. 'Sorry.'

'But this was all your idea. You, Gus and George had spoken to Wills.'

Michael looked down. 'It was mostly George and Gus, if I'm honest.'

'Yet, you went along with it. You could have said it wasn't

for you any time. I could see you were turned on last Sunday when Rachel led me into the room. You liked that, I know you did. So try and remember that, rather than Monday night. And those women, the ones you've dated, how come none of them have worked out?'

'What do you mean?'

'You don't have a girlfriend, and you said none of the women you've dated would have wanted you to do what Wills did to me on Monday. But did you ask them what they wanted in the bedroom? Or did you just wham-bam-thank-you-mam in missionary position?'

Michael flushed. 'You're very direct, Emily. But then you always were.'

'Wills told me it was you who said I needed taking down a peg or two, Michael. So don't go blaming everything on George and Gus.'

Michael clenched his jaw. 'You do, Emily, and I hope whatever George and Gus do, you'll feel really humiliated, like I do right now, because of the way you've treated me.'

Emily got up from her chair behind the desk and bent over it, looking at him sideways she licked her lips and pouted. 'Come on, Michael. Whatever happens with George and Gus will be out of your hands. You're the one who wants to punish me. Yet, when you had the chance, you didn't. What's stopping you?'

Michael swallowed.

Emily walked over to him. She pulled his tie loose and stroked the top of his shirt, then moved slowly down his body until she came to his swollen cock. 'What are you thinking? That you could use this tie to bind my hands together, bend me over the desk, lift up my skirt and teach me how to be nicer to you.'

Michael grabbed her by her arms, spun her round and pushed her towards the desk. He groaned when he lifted up her skirt and exposed her scantily-clad butt and thighs adorned with lace-topped stockings.

'Come on, Michael, make my arse pink,' Emily purred. She wiggled her buttocks, tempting him.

He took off his belt and struck her hard.

'Whoa there, tiger, don't tear the skin. The pleasure is to take it slowly, enjoy it.'

He brought the belt down again.

Emily moaned with pleasure. 'Better.'

Michael gasped, unzipped his trousers, and spilled his cum over her arse.

'What will you tell Wills?' Michael asked, after they had both cleaned up and dressed.

Emily poured them each a whisky and smiled. 'That you challenged yourself to a do-over. He'll be sorry he missed it.'

Michael sipped on the whisky. 'His presence might have been part of the problem.'

'What if it had been Rachel who had strapped me to the board last night?'

Michael flushed.

Emily nodded. 'Got it. Even though Wills wasn't here today, I will describe everything that happened. He'll be turned on, and then he'll fuck me.'

'Wow.' Michael raised his glass towards her. 'I hate to admit it, but I'm jealous of what you two have.'

'Our choices aren't for everyone, but I hope you find someone who will make you as happy as Wills makes me. And don't be afraid of asking her what she wants, when you meet her.

You might be surprised.'

George

Emily watched Wills put some of her favourite teasing toys in a bag. It was Saturday morning, and he'd got her out of bed unusually early. The trial had concluded the day before.

Following her intervention on Wednesday, Michael had redeemed himself as prosecuting council. His closing argument was impressive. As Emily predicted, Wills enjoyed her account of what happened between her and Michael, and he'd fucked her brains out.

'No breakfast,' she whined.

'I've made it to-go. It's all ready,' he said. 'Wear this.'

'Really?' Emily wrinkled her nose at the tacky PVC dress that laced across the front.

Wills eyed her. 'Are you going to be difficult?'

She giggled. 'Yeah, especially cos this is George.'

Wills smiled. 'I've told you it will be fun. All the elements you like, dress up and lots of restraint. Rachel is coming too, to help. Are you OK with that?'

'Yeah, yeah of course,' she said and shivered when she saw Wills selecting a fitted bondage mask for her to wear. They hadn't practised total enclosure play for a while.

They picked up Rachel and drove out of London. The autumn trees were abundant with red, burnished-gold and yellow leaves. Emily devoured the wrap Wills had filled with Mexican tofu scramble and avocado. 'Delicious, my love,' she said, moving closer to him and kissing his cheek. She might not have been looking forward to indulging George, but she was happy that Rachel was there. Her tummy was tight with excitement that Rachel and Wills might both be participating.

They had been driving for about an hour when Wills pulled over. 'Put this on,' he said, handing her the hood. Rachel helped her coil her hair and zipped the hood into position.

Emily shivered when she felt the leather cuffs on each of her wrists locked together in front of her. Wearing the hood was stimulating, and she was already close to orgasm.

Wills started the car again, but they hadn't travelled far when he stopped. The car door opened and Emily was pulled roughly out of the passenger seat. She evaluated the ground with her feet. She could hear birds and a faint rustle of leaves as the gentle breeze moved through the trees. Without warning, she felt herself tightly pinned between two bodies and escorted. She guessed Wills and George were the ones walking her. They walked her fast; her pencil-thin heels were difficult to manage.

'Keep up,' said a voice from behind. It was Rachel.

Emily heard a door open, then close behind them. Her escorts still gripped her tightly. They were inside now. She wanted to ask where they were. But the restrictive hood demanded silence.

'Raise your arms, then turn round,' said George.

Emily obeyed, lifting her cuffed wrists above her head. She heard the click of a lock as the cuffs were attached, pulling her upright, stretching her. She thought about the different devices Wills and she had discussed adding to their collection, trying to figure out what she was attached to and whether she was going to be suspended.

Someone undid the laces of the dress, exposing her breasts; nipple clamps were fastened, pinching her. The back of her dress was raised, and a paddle struck her naked butt. Unlike Michael, George was not tentative. She could tell he was enjoying this, and despite her feelings about George, she was enjoying it, too. She gasped, ready to come.

'Not yet,' said Rachel. 'Control it.'

Emily guessed she and Wills were holding up the skirt of her dress.

'Open your legs,' said George.

Emily obeyed, wondering how long she could hold the orgasm while George licked her breasts and fingered her. Her body betrayed her, and she shook with pleasure.

'Failed,' said George. 'Remove the clamps and her dress. Next station.' His voice was assertive, clipped. He reminded Emily of a brusque policeman she'd had to deal with when she first practised law. The officer hadn't covered himself in glory. The way he'd treated a woman up on charges for burglary had resulted in the case being dismissed.

The next 'station' turned out to be a St. Andrews Cross. Wherever they were was very well equipped. The cross needed height, if she was going to be rotated.

She was strapped facing the cross inwards, so she knew that he was going to flog or whip her. If George's purpose were to see how much punishment she could take without a climax, this was not a good choice. Just being on the device was exhilarating as she was rotated, suspended upside-down, teased then rotated again. The flogger stung when it landed on the top of her thighs and her butt..

After five or six strokes, she heard George groan. He was going to come before she did this time. She heard a door close. After a few minutes, Rachel spoke.

'I'm going to remove the bondage hood. George needs time to sort himself out, and you've worn that long enough. Do you feel OK, if George wants to continue?'

'I'm having a blast,' Emily said when Rachel took off the hood. 'What happened to George?'

'You were too much for him, you sexy redhead,' Wills said, slapping her bottom.

'Do that again. I'm thinking we should get one of these for our house.'

Rachel tutted. 'Poor George. He had it planned out so perfectly. Your humiliation, how you would be begging him to stop and release you.'

'Yeah, well, he chose some pretty exciting equipment – or was that you, Rachel, giving him a bum steer?'

'His choice to come here. This is the family estate, apparently, and he owns all the stuff. The house is well-equipped and rivals serious BDSM play party locations from what I've seen.'

'Wills, if you're not going to spank my arse, can you unstrap me, so at least I can look around? See what else he's got for pleasure.'

Wills fondled her butt cheeks. 'No, I think I'm going to leave you here for a bit. I like the view, and maybe George will let me have a turn with you. Rachel, do you want to take a look around with me?'

Emily already knew he would be enjoying seeing her suspended and immobilised. He often left her strapped between the posts of their bed while he read the paper or suspended her in the swing on the bedroom door, while he watched a film. She was enjoying being strapped to the device too much to really want to be released.

'Come back soon and show me how this thing really works.' She was lost in thought about the possibilities the device offered when she heard George come back into the room.

He was shouting at her. His language was foul and personally abusive.

Emily tensed; there was no way she could defend herself if he went through with what he was threatening. She yelped as a horse whip tore into her flesh. 'Wills, Rachel, help me!' she screamed.

'Shut up,' said George, taping her mouth closed before she could scream again.

Almost at once, Wills and Rachel ran into the room. 'Put that down, George,' demanded Wills.

'She asked for it,' he said, and thrashed Emily across the back for the second time.

Emily was terrified, helplessly restrained, listening to the kerfuffle: flesh against flesh, then the sound of glass breaking.

'You'll pay for that,' George whimpered. When Wills took another swipe at him, he fled.

Rachel released Emily and carefully removed the tape from her mouth. She wrapped her in a rug and led her out of the room. 'Here, darling,' she said, handing Emily a bag containing a dress, makeup, and jewellery.

'Why did you bring this?'

'Actually, it was your husband. He's booked a table to treat us all to a fancy dinner afterwards. The PVC dress wouldn't have passed muster.'

Emily laughed. 'Definitely. I'm guessing George choose that PVC thing, by the way? It wasn't one of ours?'

'Yep.'

'Bloody typical. Probably gets his rocks off on really bad porn.'

'Worse than that, I think he's really turned on by abusing women and causing actual pain. That whip he used on you is something no one who would ever use on human flesh for pleasure. He's dangerous. It's how things go horribly wrong. I probably should have guessed when he asked for you to wear the hood. He wanted to dehumanise you.'

Wills came and scooped Emily into his arms. 'Oh, my darling, I'm so sorry.'

Emily kissed him. 'It's not your fault. We did get to try out something new.'

'Isn't my wife wonderful?' Wills asked Rachel.

'She's a treasure, Wills. You're a lucky man.'

Emily snuggled into him and pulled the blanket around her. 'I don't want to get changed here, if that's OK. Let's go home first and see how we're all doing.'

Despite the horrible ending to the afternoon, after the drive home and freshening up, Emily told Wills she would still like a night out.

A journalist friend had helped Wills secure a table at a four-star Michelin restaurant. Wills kept the location as a surprise until their taxi arrived.

Emily wore a shiny lilac Vivienne Westwood, Rachel a deep blue vintage dress complete with bustier and Wills a dark green satin shirt with patent Jimmy Choo's on his feet. They made a spectacular trio as they entered the restaurant.

'I feel like I'm back in my courtroom,' Emily whispered to Rachel, noticing the other diners staring at them while the maître d' showed them to their table.

'Yeah, you're certainly good at making an entrance. We should have included a collar tonight.'

Emily laughed.

'Behave, you two,' said Wills as they sat. He asked Rachel to choose from the wine list. 'Anything you like,' he said.

Rachel selected a Viognier and a white Rioja. 'Either of these will be delicious for white and either the Masato or Chateau Lafite for red. I thought you had to book months ahead to eat here.'

'They keep last minute reservations a bit of a secret. A few spots are always open for celebrity guests, and my friend has an in with the owner. Shall we start with a champagne cocktail?'

The women studied the menu while Wills ordered the cocktails. There were two choices in each of the menu sections for Emily, who had become a vegan after she and Wills married.

'What was that about a collar for Ems?' Wills asked, grinning. 'You're right. I wish I'd thought of it, the way everyone was staring.'

'Haha, Wills, that would have needed the rubber Westwood, which I don't have.'

'Yet,' said Wills and winked.

The banter about what Emily would and would not like to wear continued throughout dinner. Rachel offered up some interesting vintage suggestions and where they could buy them. 'I think something like that might work well for your next scenario, with Gus.'

Emily raised her eyebrows. 'Do say more. I love corsets.'

Wills shook his head at Rachel. '*Don't* say any more. She's a minx and will guess.'

Emily put her head on one side. 'Well, despite the debacle of what happened today, I'm looking forward to the next one.' She smiled coquettishly at Wills, who reached over the table and took her hand.

When they arrived home, Wills helped Emily out of the dress. He rubbed salve on the wounds George had made with the whip, and then he made love to her on the soft cream rug in their bedroom.

'I love you, Ems,' he whispered into her ear. Her body writhed in pleasure beneath him as he brought her to a second orgasm.

'Hmm, for missionary sex, that was pretty amazing,' she purred.

Later, when they were in bed, Wills read while she listened to a podcast. Sensing something was troubling her husband, she took out her earbuds and touched his hand. 'What's the matter?'

Wills shook his head. 'Nothing.'

'That's like saying you're fine when you're bleeding from a cut. Tell me.'

He sighed and put his book on the bedside table. 'I didn't protect you today. I didn't keep you safe. That welt on your back – it's my fault, and it should never have happened. I shouldn't have left you. I was being selfish. I left you there because I wanted to fuck you on that contraption. Now I never want to see one again.' His words tumbled out, no longer able to control his anguish. He sobbed loudly.

Emily held him and stroked his hair. 'None of today was your fault. George chose to do what he did. And God knows, I feel concerned knowing he invites and pays women to go there so he *can* hurt them. That's why he has all that equipment. It's not for mutual pleasure, but for his sadism. He's a small man, an abuser. I never want to see him again.'

Wills nodded. 'How come none of us realised what he was really like?'

'Abusers are cunning. Did you know the trial is about a dead sex worker? She died in hospital after a so-called bad date. The man up on charges is a respectable married man with three children and a house in the suburbs.'

Wills nodded. 'George could end up on charges like that one day.'

'Yeah, or worse. He could end up killing a girl. I'd like to be the one to sentence him, but more importantly, he needs to be stopped. Will you talk to him?'

'Yes, and I'm going to tell both Michael and Gus what happened. Are you alright with that? They should know too.'

'Yes, of course. You know, I've always figured he was a creep.'

Gus

After four days of deliberation, the jury brought in a verdict of not guilty just before lunch the following Thursday. Gus had presented a reasonable and factual defence. Several members of the jury didn't warm to Michael's arguments about the dead girl being a victim. They saw her as a stereotypical example of someone who had chosen a life with significant risk. 'In other words, to some of our jurors, she deserved it,' sighed Emily to Glenda.

'She didn't seem to have anyone who cared much about her, apart from her friend.'

'And the way she presented… It gave the jury even more reason not to see what had really gone on. Merciless brutality, disguised as an accident.' Emily thought about George and shuddered.

'His wife was very convincing.'

'Wasn't she just. He'd probably asked her to try out some of his kink fetishes and she'd refused. Drink?' Emily held up a bottle of sherry and pointed to a bottle of whisky.

'Thanks, but no. I'm heading off to yoga. The two don't mix.'

'Quite right. I should follow your example, but I have…' She swept her hand over the desk of papers she needed to read, including a bundle for the next trial she would be presiding over. 'Enjoy your long weekend.'

Emily had just poured herself a sherry when her phone rang. It was Rachel. 'I'm about to order a taxi and head over to your chambers. Can you leave in half an hour? Gus told Wills the trial was finally over.'

'Oh bless him, no, I have a ton of paperwork and reading to do. How long can I delay? I'm guessing the Gus scenario is planned for tonight.'

'I think he wants to celebrate his win, and we have a train to catch. The latest you'll be able to delay is four o'clock.'

'For heaven's sake. Not that I agree with the verdict, personally.'

'He might be a little less celebratory, now. He and Michael are meeting with Wills. Wills is talking to them about George.'

'Good. George has called Wills three times this week. Fucking nerve. He ghosted him, but George is saying he'll try to pin an assault charge on Wills.'

'How? That's rubbish.'

'Indeed. I'm just hoping he doesn't go to the police. The press would have a field day with the story, because George is not going to be shy about disclosing what we were all doing there. I'll be ready to leave by the time you get here, but whatever is happening, I have nothing to change into here.'

'All taken care of. See you soon.'

Emily's eyes glazed over as she tried to concentrate on her reading for the next trial. Wills was still blaming himself about what had happened, and she was surprised that he'd agreed to go ahead with Gus so quickly. But maybe this was what they all needed. Some fun to put the events of last Saturday into perspective. She checked herself in the mirror and freshened her makeup. She always kept it to a minimum for court, but she loved bright lipsticks and eyeliner when she was dressing to go anywhere. She laughed when she saw the size of the suitcase Rachel had with her in the back of the taxi. 'You did come prepared. Is half our bedroom in there?'

'Almost. The hotel Wills has booked is grand, though I doubt the bedrooms are equipped for what Gus has planned.'

'What on earth did you suggest? And how come we're going to a hotel?'

'Your husband added a little extra to the original scenario. He wanted to make sure you had time to relax, too, so we're staying over until Saturday. The hotel has a spa.'

Emily patted Rachel's arm. 'I'm glad you were free to come. How's the new manager for the wine bar working out?'

'He's great, hence my availability. I'd like to have you both over for dinner to meet him. Next week, if you're free.'

'Ah, so is he more than just a manager?'

Rachel winked. 'Endless possibilities, which is how he got the job.' She handed Emily a box. 'This is for you to change into when we get to the station. The men are meeting us there at the bar.'

Once there, Emily made her way to the ladies' toilet and changed into the clothes Rachel had picked out for her. A cream satin corset, sheer stockings, a vintage navy and white full-flared cocktail dress and dark blue stiletto court shoes.

'Audrey Hepburn eat your heart out,' said Rachel as she helped Emily pin her hair into a pleat.

Emily did a quick shimmy when she joined Wills and Gus at the bar. 'Close your mouth, Wills. It's me, your wife.'

'God, you're beautiful,' he said.

Emily turned and allowed Gus to peck her cheek. She held onto him for a moment and whispered, 'I'm looking forward to this.'

Gus swallowed and looked back at Wills. 'Can't we just stay here, mate? I mean…'

Wills laughed. 'It'll be worth the wait, I promise.'

Rachel and Emily exchanged glances. 'Don't ask me for details,' Rachel said. 'I think I'm out of the loop.'

Emily sat next to Wills as the train sped through the outskirts of London into the Kent countryside. She rested her head on his shoulder and stretched her legs under the table. Looking at Gus, she rubbed her foot against his calf and smiled. 'So, how bad have I been, in your opinion?'

Gus adjusted his tie and coughed. 'You'll have to wait and see, Mrs William Hawkins. Your husband is also not terribly pleased with your antics recently.'

'Ooh,' said Emily. 'A double flogging. How delicious.'

Gus shook his head, gave a suppressed laugh, and shrugged. 'She's incorrigible, Wills.'

Wills nodded, then stared at the passenger sitting across the aisle, who had smiled after Emily's comment about a double flogging. He was clearly tuned into their conversation. Wills put his arm around Emily. The passenger looked away, scrolling through his phone.

Emily reassured her husband with her hand and whispered, 'It's OK, Wills, you don't need to worry. He's just a nosy parker.'

While Emily and Wills relaxed, Rachel and Gus spent the rest of the journey chatting about travel and her knowledge of wine:

which wine regions she'd visited and her plans to expand her wine collection. Emily noted that Rachel gave little away about her personal life to anyone other than her. Gus would have no idea about Rachel's regular travels to exclusive bondage parties in the UK, Europe and other more exotic locations.

The spa hotel was a few miles from Dover. A converted castle, with tastefully designed landscaping.

Wills had booked a suite for himself and Emily, along with two separate rooms for Gus and Rachel. The main suite was furnished with a four-poster bed, chaise, couch, desk, dining table and various chairs.

Wills checked his watch. 'Who's hungry?'

Everyone raised their hands.

'Actually,' said Emily, 'do you mind if I have a quiet word with Wills before we go to dinner? Maybe meet you both in the bar in half an hour?'

Gus nodded. 'Sure.'

Emily sat on the couch and patted the cushion next to her. She took Wills hand.

'What's up, Ems?'

'Not me, you. I could tell how much that creep on the train unsettled you; plus you were talking about George to Michael and Gus earlier. You seem stirred up.'

Wills stroked her cheek and nuzzled her hair. 'You know me so well. It's not just George. Something you said a while ago, that you were worried about us being not enough for each other if we involved other people. And...' He ran his hands through his hair. 'I'm the one who suggested it.'

Emily frowned. 'And I agreed. In fact, I pushed you into it, in a way.'

'You didn't. I was excited, and I wanted you to have fun.

You're one full-on lady, and I love you for it. But last Saturday... and yeah, that man on the train, when I saw him listening in and ogling you...' Wills shrugged.

Emily kissed him. 'We can just enjoy a weekend away. Gus will understand. He's a good friend.'

'Yeah, but he's been desperate to get into your knickers since college. And he nearly did!'

Emily pulled a sad face, then grinned. 'But he didn't.'

'But you fancy him, right?'

'Yeah, he's lovely. Those grey-green eyes and his cheeky East London accent, which he exaggerates or manages to lose completely when it suits him. He's a charmer, Wills, but it's you I love. And we can call everything to a halt right now, if you want. You can say I'm not up for it.'

Wills stood, pulling Emily with him. 'Thank you, sweet lady, but I'll be fine, so long as you are. Let's go find our playmates and eat dinner. I'm starving.'

Emily rose up to kiss him on the cheek; despite her heels, at six-foot-two, he was still a good eight inches taller. 'You always make me feel safe. Never forget that.'

By the time they joined Rachel and Gus in the bar, Emily could see Wills was more relaxed. The banter between him and Gus during dinner even made Rachel blush.

Wills and Gus prepared the suite, then sat on the couch to watch Rachel undress Emily and fix her with a leash.

Rachel took her time with each of the buttons before removing the dress and parading Emily in front of the men. Emily's breasts spilled over the half-cups of the boned corset that cinched her waist. Rachel led Emily over to the foot of the four-poster bed, fastened her hands and feet to either side of the bed posts, covered her eyes with a mask, then stepped away.

Emily held her breath, wondering what was going to happen next. She loved the sensation of the straps holding her firmly in place. She was wet, longing for contact, for touch, for the stings of the flogger or crop. She was about to beg when she heard the swish and felt the strands of the two floggers, one straight after the other.

'You said severe, right?' said Gus.

Emily's stomach fluttered at the sound of his voice and the sting from each time the floggers connected to her flesh.

He stopped, and she felt him standing right behind her. His hands moved around the front of her body, cupping and massaging her, moving down from her breasts to her buttocks, probing her, running his fingers over her swollen clitoris.

After that, Emily didn't know whose hands were whose. The back of her corset was unhooked. She felt the floggers drag over her upper thighs, her breasts, her sides and her stomach, as if each of her tormentors were following a beat. One, two, three, repeat. She opened her mouth and gasped. Wills had teased with two floggers on occasion, but three was intense, almost more than she could bear, yet she wanted to bear it. She tried to imagine who was where. She was powerless to stop the orgasm exploding inside her. She exhaled.

She loved the sensation of being physically powerless by consent. Straining against her bondage, unable to writhe, she moaned loudly while hands explored her, lips kissed her and fingers probed her. A lubricated dildo was pushed into her anus, a tongue explored her labia and sucked on her clit. Thighs on either side of her face, then a cock in her mouth, while another mouth sucked on her nipples and licked her breasts. Every orifice and nerve ending was satiated. Someone started manipulating the dildo, and a second cock filled her cunt, pumping her hard before filling her with cream. Emily whimpered, the sensation of complete satisfaction, beyond anything she'd ever felt or experienced before.

Wills removed the eye mask and was about to release her from the bed when she asked, 'What about Rachel?'

'I'm here darlin', what do you need?'

'Nothing, I meant...'

Rachel put up a hand to stop her. 'I'm absolutely fine. Gus and Wills saw how much pleasure I got from the experience. And my bar manager will be online with me later, so I'm good.'

'But, I mean, if you want to... I'm still all tied up.'

'What you are is insatiable,' said Rachel. She wiped Emily's face and bent down to kiss her on the forehead tenderly. 'We have a good friendship, that's all I need.'

Emily smiled. 'OK. In that case, continue releasing me, husband.'

'I will, but I have to warn you, your freedom is only temporary,' Wills laughed. 'For now, though, we all deserve a shower and a big nightcap. Then I've more fun planned for you, wife.'

Emily raised her eyebrows and clapped her hands.

When Rachel and Gus left, Wills kept his promise, gagging her and strapping her to the end of the bed. He lay down opposite her, scrolling through his phone and ignoring her attempts to make eye contact. When he could see she was almost ready to come, he removed the gag, picked up the whip he'd placed by the bed earlier and used it on her butt.

'Who came in your mouth?' he asked, swishing the whip against her upper thigh.

Emily pouted. 'Of course I know,' she said.

Wills used the whip again, harder this time. 'Tell me.'

She winced. 'Gus,' she said.

Wills didn't speak. He released her from the bed posts and fingered her until she came. He finished himself over her breasts and face.

Despite her cajoling, Wills didn't join her in the shower. Emily felt guilty. Why hadn't she known whether it was Wills or Gus in her mouth? Surely Wills wouldn't have allowed Gus to fuck her. She gasped. Had everything gone too far, spoiled what they'd had? When Wills picked up the whip, his eyes had been cold, like he meant to hurt her – the way George had.

Penitence

Emily took Rachel to one side when they met for breakfast the following morning. Wills had risen early and gone for a run.

'I need to know who was where yesterday. Did Wills fuck me? Please, it's important.'

Rachel bit her lip. 'I'm not going to ask why you need to know, but how will you feel if it wasn't Wills?'

Emily gasped. 'So it was Gus?'

Rachel nodded. 'Sorry. Shit, I tried to remind them both what they'd agreed to. But I saw Gus check with Wills, and Wills gave him the nod… I mean, the whole scenario was pretty mad and intense.'

Emily swallowed. 'Yeah, it was exciting, but Wills is…' Why had Wills allowed her to think she'd given him the right answer? What was he planning to do now?

'What happened after we left?' Rachel asked.

Emily told her. Then, 'At law school, after I kissed Gus – it was a drunk snog, really – Wills broke up with me for about two weeks. Then he came my room, apologised, and we were back together. I can't believe that he set it up so Gus was the one to fuck me. Wills was already in my mouth.'

'You're going to have to talk to him,' Rachel said. 'You can't let this fester. I'm sorry I didn't do more. Wills told me he didn't want Gus to fuck you, the same way you asked him not to fuck me when we first met, but I assumed he'd changed his mind.'

Emily closed her eyes, her cheeks pale. She stumbled, feeling faint.

'Here, sit down, take a deep breath.'

'Everything alright?' Wills asked having returned from his run. Rachel and Emily sat down at the table. Gus was engrossed in the Saturday Papers. Wills drummed the table lightly and looked around. 'Beautiful day, perfect for another surprise for my beautiful wife.'

'Stop it, Wills,' said Emily.

Wills put his head on one side. 'Stop what?'

'I think you and I need to talk.'

Gus put the paper down. 'What's happening?'

Wills clenched his jaw and stared at Emily. 'My wife has changed her mind, it seems. Sorry about that, Gus.' He rose from the table and headed into the lobby of the hotel.

Gus pulled a face and opened his hands. 'I don't have a clue what's happening.'

'Yeah, you do, Gus,' Emily snapped. She followed Wills back to their room.

Wills was standing by the window, clicking his fingers and counting. It was something he used to do to calm himself down before an exam. She hadn't seen him use the technique for years.

She sat on the couch in the sitting area. She knew he needed to find his equilibrium before she tried to talk to him. Her phone buzzed; it was a text from Rachel. *Gus and I will check out, leave you two to sort things.*

The rooms are paid for until tomorrow. Just enjoy the spa, book a treatment if you want. I might need a friend. Please stay

OK. Stay in touch, let me know when you two have talked.

Emily was relieved to have a friend close by in case Wills took off. She knew she wouldn't want to go to their house if they couldn't manage to clear this mess up. She stared at her husband's back, willing him to look around and speak to her.

Eventually, Wills moved away from the window and sat opposite her. The tension between them was a million miles from the electric excitement of when they'd sat on that couch the night before.

'Why did you let Gus…? I mean, you told Rachel you didn't want him to.'

'I thought *you'd* realise and stop it.'

Emily shook her head. 'How? Do you have any idea what I was experiencing last night? I loved being part of something exciting that we'd both agreed to. You were the one who, for whatever reason, appears to have made up some arbitrary measure of what I was supposed to know. Rachel saw you give Gus permission. She saw Gus check with you. You're being unreasonable, Wills. Cruel, actually.'

'You think *I'm* cruel, after everything you've put me through?'

'What have I put you through, exactly? Being a loving wife who enjoys sex and games and having fun?'

Wills sighed.

'Does this go back to law school?'

'All I know is I can't unsee what I saw – how much you were enjoying him. So now I know I'm not enough for you. As you predicted.'

'That's rubbish. Do you want to know what I've learned?' She got up, sat at his feet, and took his hands into hers. 'I love you more than anything. More than anyone in the world, Wills. I'm not like Rachel. The idea of partying with others continually – it's not for me. *You* are. Our games, where you're in control and I make up stories, where you get turned on by watching me tied up, where you talk about what you'd like to do with other women. Let's go back to that.'

'It won't be enough for you, Ems. Not after yesterday.'

'How dare you tell me that you know what I want better than I know it myself? OK, have it your way. Sulk. Play the victim. You set this in motion, and you know, I told you yesterday, you could have stopped this at any time. You chose what happened last night. Don't put your guilty feelings on me and claim that your change of mind is my fault!'

Emily went to the bathroom. She changed into a bathing costume and the hotel's towelling robe, messaged Rachel, then made her way to the pool. She dove in and started swimming length after length, until she felt the anger dissipate. She clung onto the edge of the pool and breathed deeply.

'Impressive,' said Rachel.

'Needed,' said Emily. 'Now I need a massage, if they have a spot open.'

'How's Wills?'

'Sulking. Where's Gus?'

'He left, caught the next train back to the smoke. He thought it was best.'

'Poor chump. That's a fence Wills will have to mend.'

'Didn't you realise he's deeply in love with you? He sobbed like a baby last night, after we left your room. Spent the night with me. Not...' Rachel flung her hands in the air. 'I was Mummy. Which is sad, because I'm not *that* old.'

Emily snorted. 'You should have told me this morning. Sorry, I made everything about me when we spoke earlier.'

Rachel glanced over to the pool room door. 'Here's Wills. I'll leave you. I'll be in the hot tub.'

Emily stiffened as Wills swam across to join her.

'My Lady Judge, beautiful wife, lover. Will you forgive me?'

Emily paused, looking into his eyes to see if he was really penitent. She found him so. 'Of course, but only after I've sentenced you,' she giggled.

'What do you have in mind?'

'There's a woman who needs to be taught a lesson. Her behaviour has been, well, let's say, a disgrace to womanhood. I think you're the man for the job.'

Wills put an arm round her and reached down, pushing his fingers inside the gusset of her swimsuit. 'Can I start immediately?'

'Do ten lengths and then join me,' she said. She jumped up from the pool and made her way back to the suite to shower.

When Wills joined her, he found his wife sitting at the dining table wearing a collar, blindfold, garter belt, stockings and shoes. On the table there were two floggers, cuffs, straps, a riding crop and a wand.

'Stand up,' Wills said, and he bent her over the top of the table. He attached the ankle and wrist cuffs to the collar, fastened her hands behind her and strapped her legs apart, across the width of the table.

Emily purred softly as she heard the swish of the crop. Wills double-flogged her until she begged him to fuck her.

'I don't think you deserve that yet,' he said, leaving her strapped to the table.

Moments later, she felt the warm jelly fingered into her anus, and then metal as he inserted a training hook and attached it to the collar.

Emily let out a moan.

'What do you say?'

'Please, sir.'

'No,' said Wills and flogged her again. 'Now what do you say?'

'Sorry, sir.'

'Better. But not humble enough.'

'I'm truly sorry, master.' Emily didn't know how much longer she could hold her climax. The thrill of his control over her, her immobility…

'Better,' he said, teasing her with the wand. 'Don't come.'

But Emily was too aroused; the orgasm bolted through her.

Wills unstrapped her from the table and instructed her to crawl over to the bed. He stretched her diagonally, strapping her hands and feet to the top and bottom posts. The anal hook jolted her each time she moved.

'Please, master,' she begged, then groaned as he walked away smiling and went to take a shower.

The Debrief

They had been back from the spa for three days, and Emily had started presiding at the new trial.

'How did it go?' Emily asked when Wills returned from meeting with Gus.

'Let's just say, our friendship won't ever be the same again. Gus said everything was fine, but I know it's not, really.'

'I feel horrible. I've treated him badly over the years. I see that now – the way I kept teasing and flirting with him. But I didn't realise how he really felt about me.'

'Who doesn't fall in love with you, Ems? A little trail of broken hearts wherever you go. Even Rachel loves you.'

'Silly, she's a good friend. And I don't break hearts. I've been with you since I was twenty-one for heaven's sake. Ten years.'

'Minus two weeks.' Wills winked.

'You're the only one for me, Wills, for always,' she said, and kissed him.

'For always, Ems,' said Wills. 'Now about that game of enclosure we haven't played for a while…' He reached into their dressing up trunk for a silver gimp suit and hood.

Seven

Climax

Throughout our marriage, I'd blamed Jack for not being exciting, but deep down, I knew I could have stopped playing the fragile princess and been honest with him. I hadn't married him for love; I'd married him to escape, and I'd used him. Leaving him would have been kinder for both our sakes. Accepting blame for how things turned out didn't come easily. I felt ashamed.

I remembered going late-night shopping with a friend from work, not long after Jack and I left the church. We ventured into the lingerie section of a posh department store and giggled as we perused the selection of satin camisoles, suspenders and teddies on display. My friend dared me to try on a dark blue teddy, trimmed with cream lace. It had snappers to open the crotch. It was a far cry from the nighties that Jack had bought me, and I'd loved the feeling when I looked in the mirror, holding my hair up, posing, mouth open and sultry, like the pictures of the women modelling the lingerie. But unlike my friend, who left the store with a full bag of nightwear, I didn't buy the teddy.

I closed the Kindle and turned out the light, trying to reclaim the positive outlook I'd had when I saw the shooting star. 'If your life remains grey from now on, you'll have nobody but yourself to blame,' I told myself.

That night my dreams took me on a journey through my favourite childhood books. I was Alice following the white rabbit, Lucy Pevensie having tea with Mr. Tumnus, Dorothy fleeing from the witch. As each of my personas changed, a man with a ruddy face wearing red robes and a wig banged a gavel on the pub bar, shouting, 'GUILTY.' When I woke up, my duvet was half off the bed, and I felt as if I'd been in the ring with Mike Tyson.

I'd only just stepped out of the shower when Peter arrived. 'Sorry,' I said, clutching my sensible dressing gown around me, 'can I make you a tea or coffee while I get organised? Bad night, and…' I shrugged, embarrassed by my appearance.

He smiled. His eyes were soft, non-judgemental. 'It's no problem, take your time. I'll help myself to a coffee, if that's alright.'

'Through here.' I ushered him into the kitchen. 'I'll be down in less than ten minutes.'

'Have you had breakfast?'

'I'll grab a piece of toast and some fruit to eat on the way, if that's alright,' I said, and I ran upstairs to finish dressing. By the time I came down, Peter had toast and perfectly cooked scrambled eggs topped with slices of avocado ready on a plate for me.

'Sit, relax,' he said, pouring me a coffee from the cafetière.

'Thank you, this is... wait, I didn't even *have* an avocado.'

'I did. I picked up some groceries for our picnic. You look stressed. What's up?'

'I had a bit of a revelation about myself. It's not pleasant to realise you've been deliberately unkind. And that it's too late to do anything about it.'

He sat across the table and inclined his head. 'Want to talk about it?'

I didn't *want* to tell him, but the words spilled out: 'I guess every marriage has its secrets. I blamed Jack for not making ours exciting enough for me. I realise now I was just as responsible for how it ended up. Jack dealt with a lot of selfish behaviours that most men would have walked away from.'

'When you brought him to Christmas and summer work functions, we all saw how much he loved you,' said Peter. 'Sounds to me like you're being very hard on yourself. Grief does that.'

'This isn't grief talking, I...' I began ugly crying uncontrollably. Gasping for breath, I grabbed for a tissue. Red, smudged eyes and a snotty nose wasn't exactly the look I'd been hoping for when I did my makeup.

Peter reached his hand across the table. 'Crying is good. Let it go.'

A man who wasn't afraid of tears, I marvelled, dabbing my cheeks with the tissue and trying to get feelings under control. 'I'll just repair the damage,' I said, circling my face with my index finger.

He walked over to my side of the table. 'Would a hug help?'

I trembled as I stood up and felt his arms around me. Pulling my head into his chest, he stroked my hair.

When I lifted my face to his, he bent down, put his mouth

over mine and kissed me gently. I didn't pull away. He held me closer. I put my arms around him and melted. His body was firm, lean and toned. I sighed when he began to massage my breasts over the fabric of my top.

'Is this alright, Allison?' he whispered.

'Yes,' I whispered, 'but not here.' I took his hand and led him upstairs to my bedroom.

'Are you sure?' he asked, watching me unbutton my top and stretch out on my bed.

'Oh yes,' I said, beckoning him to join me. He removed my bra and his shirt then lay over me, skin to skin. He kissed my neck and breasts. Opening my shorts, he kissed my tummy and moved slowly down to my labia.

I moaned softly while his tongue explored me and his fingers made their way inside my vagina. 'I want you,' I whispered.

He moved skilfully, teasing me with his fingers and kissing my flesh before he took me. He entered me slowly at first, then harder, encouraging my moans and waiting for my response. I climaxed before he came. He waited, holding me, peppering my face with light kisses. 'Are you alright?' he whispered, lying next to me.

'So much more than alright,' I said.

He raised himself onto his elbows and studied my face.

'I've never... never had an orgasm like that before,' I told him, flushing, turning my face away.

He leaned down and kissed my cheek. 'I'm surprised. You seemed so confident, when you lay on the bed.'

I laughed. 'Confident, if only. Except you...' I stopped unsure what to tell him. The stories from the book Heather had given me had opened my mind, shown me that it was OK to make choices and physically respond to feeling sexually aroused. But

I felt nowhere near confident.

'When you started crying downstairs, I expected you to call off the day, ask me to leave. I'd like there to be more of this, if you want to.'

'I was blown away you weren't afraid of my tears. Jack was. He blamed himself when I cried, trying to fix it by leaving me alone. But if I'm honest, I used my tears to push him away.'

'Funny, Sally didn't like letting me see her cry. She always left or told me to go away.'

I smiled and kissed him again. 'Yes, to your earlier question. I'd like more of this, too. I'd also still like to go sailing – or is it too late?'

'No, let's go.'

We showered, dressed and headed off for his boat. The size of his yacht surprised me. It had two cabins, a full kitchen and a shower. I'd only ever been on a ferry, and I felt nervous as he cast off, using the motor to steer us out of the harbour.

'I'll show you what to do once we're under sail,' he said. 'And you should wear this, just in case.'

He handed me a life jacket.

'Hopefully it *is* only "just in case",' I said, fastening the orange jacket over my sweater. The sun was strong, but the temperature dropped as we left the harbour, and were soon under sail in the cool easterly wind.

He showed me the correct way to put the mooring lines around the cleats, how to steer the yacht with the tiller, how to adjust the spinnaker sheets and guys when the wind freshened and when to anticipate abandoning sailing with the spinnaker, dowsing it. By the time we returned to the harbour, my cheeks were reddened from the combination of exercise, wind and sun.

I felt exhilarated and happier than I'd been in forever. When we were back in the harbour, we sat on the deck, drinking hot chocolate from china mugs and scoffing hunks of bread, cheese, grapes and ginger biscuits from the picnic in the cooler.

'Sorry it's a bit of a random picnic,' he said.

'It's delicious. If I was stranded on a desert island, bread and cheese would be the food I wanted from home.'

'Ah, and your eight discs would be,' he chuckled, referencing the radio programme on the BBC.

I gazed out into the distance, realising how those eight discs had likely changed, in just a few short hours, except for one: Mozart's twenty-first piano concerto.

'They used it for the soundtrack to *Elvira Madigan*,' he said. 'Have you watched the film?'

'Yes, with Jack, at a special anniversary screening. Must be at least fifteen years ago. It was the only time I ever saw him cry.'

'Did you cry, too?'

I closed my eyes, guilty at the memory of leaving Jack sitting in the cinema as the credits rolled and, later, calling him a big girl's blouse. 'Yes, but I was mean to him.'

Peter took my hand, pressed it against his lips, and led me to the cabin at the front of the boat. I allowed him to undress me.

'Stand still,' he said, when I was completely naked. He stepped back and sat on the bed staring at me.

I smiled, thinking about Amirah, how she had allowed herself to be bound with rope by her lover and shivered. But I didn't dare tell him about that, not yet.

'I just wanted to take in how beautiful you are.' He stood up and wrapped me in a blanket, mistaking my shiver for cold.

'I'm not cold,' I said and pulled up his top. 'My turn to undress you.'

Our lovemaking was generous. We cherished each other, fondling, stroking, exploring. He knew exactly where and how to touch me. He kissed me everywhere, his tongue gliding over my skin as if I were edible and he was slowly savouring the taste of me. I orgasmed as soon as his tongue brushed my clitoris.

It was Heather's turn to sit with her mouth gaping open when I met up with her the following night. 'Sounds like you being in that pub was perfect synchronicity. I like your choice for the book group, by the way. A classic with contemporary issues.' She held up a well-read copy of *Madame Bovary*.

'I need to correct what I told you before, about me and Jack. I made out that he was an old fuddy duddy. But a lot of that was because of me. I contributed to the way things ended up.'

She reached out and squeezed my hand. 'Have you read "Wild Heaven" yet?'

I shook my head.

'I think that story will help you resolve some of the internalised guilt and conflict you're feeling.'

'How so?'

She shrugged. 'A bit like your choice of *Madame Bovary*, a woman manages her discontentment with affairs, but doesn't really find happiness, because she's not honest with herself.'

'Ooh, that's a bit harsh.'

Heather smiled. 'I speak as one who's been there. But, hey, it's my turn to share and tell you about what happened to me in Spain.' She poured us two more large glasses of Rioja.

'Right,' I said, clinking my glass against hers. I settled down to listen to Heather's account of her weekend. By the time she finished, I was laughing so hard my stomach hurt.

Still giggling from Heather's story and too much wine, I crawled into bed and opened my Kindle to see what the final story, 'Wild Heaven', could teach me about myself.

Eight

Wild Heaven

London 1973

'You're happy with the sign, then?'

Melody Wild nodded and clapped her hands. 'Perfectly done,' she said, taking a step back to admire the sign writer's handiwork. The Melody Wild Agency was no longer an idea dreamed up from her flat, with hushed meetings in coffee bars or restaurants. The Knightsbridge address was prestigious; all she needed now was for the pending business accounts to become reality. The article in *Campaign,* followed by a stinging and spiteful comment by the diary writer, confirmed that her ex-husband, Oliver Holmes, Chief Executive of Holmes Wendell and Wright, was furious.

1975

Melody stood at the top of the stairs leading to a hotel reception room, observing executives, clients, wives and partners mingling while ad agency chiefs discreetly hustled for new business. Her ex-husband Oliver was holding forth to a captivated group, his arm around a diminutive young brunette with large breasts. Always a boob man, Melody thought, glancing at her own magnificent, gravity-defying breasts. Lifting the hem of her long Thea Porter silk, she floated elegantly down the winding staircase and joined the soiree. Wearing a confident mask, she pretended to enjoy being defiantly single in a gaggle of couples.

'It seems you and I are both solo tonight.'

Melody inclined her head. The man in front of her was five-foot-nine, with shaggy hair, a beard and glasses. She noted his green eyes. He bore a strong resemblance to an American soap opera star, save for his Irish lilt. He was undeniably attractive, but not her type.

'Daniel, Daniel Martin,' he said. 'Would you mind if I joined your table for dinner?'

He bowed slightly and took her hand. He raised it to his lips, his green eyes concentrating on her face as he brushed the surface of her flesh with his mouth. Something about the simple and slightly old-fashioned gesture pleased her.

'If you don't mind talking business, you'd be welcome,' she said.

'I'll see you at dinner, then,' he said, disappearing as suddenly as he had arrived.

The interaction had disoriented her. When she saw Oliver making his way over, she felt unprepared for their usual battle of words.

'You look a little flushed, my dear,' he said. 'Is the change hitting you already?'

Melody had just celebrated her thirty-seventh birthday. Oliver's tone irked her as he had intended it to, but her usual quick wit failed.

'I'm surprised your latest squeeze isn't wearing her school uniform.' She smiled, but she knew her words were of no consequence to him.

'You're usually sharper than that, Melody. You're tired. I hear you're fishing in dangerous waters, having a dalliance with the younger set?'

Melody flinched. How did he know who she was sleeping with? 'My private life is none of your business,' she hissed.

She tried to walk away, but he caught her arm. 'You've got no chance of getting that new account, sweetheart. I'd cut your losses now, if I were you.'

'Oh drop dead,' she said, jerking free from his grasp.

'Melody, there you are. Shall we join the other guests at the table?' Daniel's Dublin accent cut through the tension.

'Let's,' she said, slipping her arm through his. 'Thank you. Not that I needed rescuing, but he was being a bigger jerk than usual.'

'I could tell,' said Daniel, pulling out a chair for her. 'You're in competition with his agency for a new client, from what I overheard.'

Melody nodded and shivered when Daniel's hand brushed her briefly on the shoulder to fix her wrap. 'I don't think we've met before,' she said.

He handed her a business card. 'We haven't. Your agency is growing, from what I read in *Campaign*. How about we meet to talk after dinner? I have a proposal for you. I'm staying at the hotel, in the Grosvenor Suite.'

Melody glanced down at the card. It bore his name, a telephone number and a logo she didn't recognise. She put the card in her clutch bag, intrigued whether his proposal was business or pleasure. She watched him interact with the other guests and admired the way he worked the table.

The event was due to finish at ten. Daniel leaned over to Melody and whispered, 'I hope I'll see you soon,' before standing. Claiming he needed to take a business phone call from overseas, he offered his apologies to the other guests and left the table.

Melody watched him weave his way through the dining room, smiling and stopping to shake hands with different men and women as he passed. His familiarity with clients and other executives she knew reassured her, and she decided to accept his invitation.

'You came – how delightful,' he said, ushering her inside the suite and closing the door behind her.

The reception room was chic, modern, and minimalist, with two low leather couches on either side of a coffee table, a writing desk, chair and a bar with two stools.

'Champagne?' He pointed to the ice bucket and two glasses waiting on top of the bar. 'Or would you prefer something warmer? A brandy or coffee liqueur? Please, make yourself comfortable.' He indicated one of the couches.

'Brandy, please.' She noticed him watching as she swept her hand under her hips, smoothing out her dress to sit. The height of her shoes and the side-split of the skirt offered him a glimpse of her legs when she crossed them.

'To you,' he said, handing her the glass. He sat at the opposite end of the couch, watching her while she took a sip of the brandy. 'That Thea Porter design looks well on you.'

'Thank you.' She lowered her eyes. His studious attention was unnerving; she already realised his invitation to discuss a proposal wasn't about business. 'Why did you invite me to meet you?'

'Why did you accept?' He touched her under the chin with his index finger, then gently moved her face so that it was in profile to his. 'You are an exceptionally beautiful woman. You have power, position, style and an outwardly exuded confidence. But…' He ran his fingers along her décolletage, then over the top of the dress, all the way down to her knees. 'My guess is you feel like an imposter.'

Melody shivered as his fingers moved back up the material, outlining the fullness of her breasts. Her nipples pushed against the fabric. He circled the outline of her areolae with his fingertip. Leaning forward to kiss her, he squeezed her left nipple between his thumb and forefinger.

Melody yelped.

'Close your eyes and breathe through it,' he whispered.

Melody moaned, aroused. The man who wasn't her type was dangerously sexual.

He released her, leaned back and folded his hands in his lap.

Melody laughed nervously and swallowed. 'I don't think this is for me,' she said, standing up. 'Sorry.'

'Don't be sorry, Melody. I understand.'

His relaxed acceptance confused her. She'd expected him to persuade her to stay.

As if he could read her mind, he said, 'I don't play games, Melody. The women I love and share experiences with are independent. It's up to them to choose whether they want to stay or not.'

'"Women"? You do this a lot?'

'Come now, don't be so coy. You're not that innocent. You've been married and had lovers.'

'I was a sixteen-year-old virgin when I married Oliver. I've had three lovers and a couple of holiday flings since we divorced. Not at the same time,' she added hurriedly, wondering why she'd felt the need to explain herself.

He smiled and reached for her hand. 'I'm sorry, I rushed you. I know you saw the logo on my card, which is why I thought you'd decided to accept my invitation. But I realise now you didn't know what it meant.'

'I've never seen it before.'

'Forgive me. If you stay, I can explain, tell you about my organisation. I promise nothing will happen that you don't consent to.' He let go of her hand and patted the sofa.

She hesitated momentarily. There was something about him that excited her. 'Sure, why not. Maybe I can create an ad campaign for you.' She laughed.

Daniel smiled as she sat down. 'Well, we don't advertise, but then, we don't need to. The people who become members are very discreet. That's one of the reasons Lifestyle works so well.'

'Lifestyle? What exactly do you do in this organisation?'

'I arrange introductions for like-minded individuals who are looking for more than marriage. Sometimes those introductions lead to more permanent arrangements. Some members marry, some members are couples who join together. Others are single or divorced or who, like me, prefer to remain single.'

'People pay you be their matchmaker with a series of potential partners, even the married ones? To have affairs?'

'There is an annual membership fee, but no other charge, and it's not dating in the traditional sense.'

'I'd like to get married again, or at least find someone who…'

'Who would love you the way you deserve,' he interrupted.

Melody nodded.

'Tell me why you think you haven't been satisfied by your lovers so far. Haven't they fulfilled you sexually or indulged you in your fantasies?'

'How do you know I'm not satisfied?'

'The way you looked when you stood at the top of the stairs. The way you responded to me when I pinched your nipple. You were excited by the pain. My guess is your fantasies are dark. You've never experienced them because you're afraid of what would happen if you did. The members of my organisation share those fantasies. Membership makes it safe to talk about them, experience them safely.'

She looked away, feeling her face redden. He was extremely close to the truth about the sexual fantasies she had never dared to talk about.

'You couldn't talk to your husband because he likes his women young, inexperienced and virginal. He serves himself. Giving his partner pleasure doesn't occur to him. He dates younger and younger women, yet you still compare yourself to them. I noticed you checking your breasts earlier. You deserve much more pleasure than he ever gave you.'

Melody shivered, searching his face with her eyes. He'd read her thoughts too accurately. 'Wait, did Oliver put you up to this?'

'Not at all. I came to support the charity the money is going towards. I had no intention of discussing Lifestyle with anyone I didn't already know, until I saw you.'

His voice was soothing. She relaxed into the sofa and thought about Charles, her Creative Director. She'd been sleeping with him for the past two months. He was younger, with coffee-coloured hair and olive skin. But sex with him wasn't exciting, the way she'd hoped it would be.

Daniel ran his fingers lightly along her arm. 'I can introduce you to men who will give you the type of pleasure you've always craved.'

She closed her eyes and sighed as he guided her fingers under her dress, between her thighs, and pressed them against her satin lingerie.

'Keep your eyes closed and think about what you would like me to do to you right now. Tie you up, spank you, and teach you pleasure through pain, watch you breathe through the intensity while I whip you? Would I watch you being suspended and taken by two men at a time?'

She gasped, aroused by his words; the orgasm surged through her. 'Take me,' she said.

He pushed her back onto the sofa and pulled up her gown. Holding her hands above her head, he pushed himself deep into her until she climaxed.

The following morning, dressed in a pale pink Dior shift, beige heels and nude stockings, she smiled at the feeling of the executive office chair's soft leather against her flesh. She tingled when she thought about the intensity of the orgasm she had experienced with Daniel on the sofa in the Grosvenor Suite. Distracted by the thought of his hypnotic voice, she found it hard to focus on work and jumped when her secretary buzzed through with a call.

'There's a Mr Martin on the line, do you want to talk to him?

He's not in your calendar, and you have a meeting with the creative team upstairs scheduled to start in five minutes.'

Melody's stomach leapt. 'Put him through and let Charles know I'll come upstairs as soon as possible.'

She paused after she heard the click, waiting for his salutation.

'Good morning, Melody. Are you available later, at five o'clock?'

'I have…' She looked at her calendar, tummy nervous and excited at the prospect of seeing him again. 'I could be. I'll ask my secretary to rearrange a meeting.'

'What are you wearing? Tell me everything, in detail.'

Melody described the pink shift, satin lingerie, stockings and shoes.

'It sounds charming. Is your dress suitable for a cocktail bar?'

'Yes, I can fix my face and add some accessories.'

'Good. I'll send my driver to collect you.'

He rang off before she could say anything else. She felt heady, as if a thousand butterflies were dancing inside her. Making her way in the lift to meet her creative team, she wondered how to explain her change of plans for the evening to Charles.

'How was the dinner?' Charles asked, meeting her outside the lift.

'Oh, you know, the usual chit chat, pretending and BS, but hey, it's good to be seen supporting these things.'

'I came to pick you up. You said it finished at ten, but no one knew where you were. I have something I want to ask you. How about after dinner tonight, once the clients have left?'

'You came to the hotel? We agreed on discretion, remember? And I'm afraid something has come up for tonight, so I won't be able to make the dinner. You'll be fine with the clients – one of the executives will go with you. Sorry.' Melody hoped that whatever he wanted to talk about was work-related. 'Another time.' She touched his arm and smiled.

'But, I…' Disappointment was written over his face.

'Not now, Charles,' she said.

The creative team had assembled in his office. Melody listened patiently as they took turns presenting their ideas for a campaign to win the new account. Melody's mind drifted while they showed her numerous sketches depicting different women in different kitchens, each holding a full bowl covered in cling film. The bowls were all upside-down.

Charles looked at her, waiting for her response.

Melody shook her head. 'I think it needs to be sexier.'

The creatives looked at each other. Nobody spoke for a few minutes.

'You want us to make Happy Wrap sexy? That wasn't the brief,' Charles said, looking around at his team. They all nodded, agreeing.

'Then the brief was wrong, and I'll talk to the exec. I can see you've all worked hard, but I don't think this will win us the account,' she said, her breathy voice contrasting the serious intention of her message. The campaign wasn't good enough. She swept out of the room, leaving confusion and a waft of Rive Gauche in her wake.

Charles followed her to the lift, blocking her way before the doors opened. 'What the devil was that?'

'Not now, Charles,' Melody said again. 'Go back to your team, talk to them. I'm sure when you look again, you'll come up with something amazing, not just the same-old-same-old product placement with a woman in the kitchen.'

'Then where do you suggest we position the product? In the bedroom?'

Melody laughed. 'You could be onto something, but sexy doesn't always mean the bedroom.' She thought about Daniel taking her on the sofa in the hotel suite and flushing.

'Where were you last night?'

Melody flinched. 'You know where – at the fundraising dinner.'

His walnut-brown pupils dilated with anger.

'For heaven's sake,' snapped Melody. 'Calm down and let me pass.'

Charles frowned and moved aside. 'How come no one knew where you were?'

'We'll talk about it another time,' she said as the lift doors closed. Discombobulated, she headed into her private bathroom.

She looked at herself from the side and from behind in the double mirrors. She'd told Daniel that her dress was suitable for a cocktail bar, but now she wasn't so sure. She checked her watch; it wasn't even one o'clock. She was already imagining him touching her again. The things he had whispered he wanted to do to her while he took her had only touched the beginning of the fantasies she'd kept secret for years.

She flicked her hands and splashed water on the sides of her face. 'Wake up, you have an agency to run, business to win,' she said aloud. She went back to her office.

Daniel phoned promptly at five. 'My driver's outside, in a silver-grey Bentley. I'm not free to meet you, but a very good friend and my number two in Lifestyle is going to take you for a drink. Maybe more. You can decide when you meet him.'

Melody stared at the handset and trembled. 'I'm not sure I'm ready to meet someone else that quickly.'

'That's fine. Have a drink, ask him whatever you need to know, then you can leave. He'll understand.'

Although she was disappointed not to see Daniel, the thought of meeting someone else from the organisation intrigued her. 'OK, I'll meet him. I'll let you know how it goes.'

The Bentley purred its way down Sloane Street, towards Sloane Square. Knightsbridge was busy with tourists and residents bustling in and out of the shops, sheltering from the spring shower under coloured umbrellas and transparent plastic macs. She raised her eyebrows when the car crossed the river. She didn't know any cocktail bars south of the Thames. The driver parked outside a redbrick block of mansion flats on Prince of Wales Drive. 'We'll just be a moment, madam. The other passenger is on their way.'

The man who climbed in beside her was tall and clean-shaven with a firm jaw, aquiline nose and thick dark hair lightly peppered with silver. He was mature, ageless and handsome. She noticed the ring on his right hand, engraved with the logo she had seen on Daniel's business card. He wore a gold wedding band on his left hand.

'Good evening, Melody.' His American accent was softer than those of the New York executives who'd sat at her table the night before.

'Hello,' she responded, waiting for him to tell her his name.

He instructed the driver where to take them and engaged Melody in polite small-talk while the Bentley headed back over the river and parked outside a well-known cocktail bar and restaurant on Cheyne Walk. Helping her from the car, he guided Melody inside. The bar was already busy, but her companion had reserved a corner table and seemed familiar with the maître d'.

He helped her onto the stool, ordered two dry martinis and sat opposite her. 'Do you like jazz?' he asked, when the pianist started to play.

'Some,' Melody said. 'I'm more a rock and roll fan. Sorry, but I don't know your name. Daniel didn't say.'

'What else didn't Daniel tell you?' He leaned forward across the table, searching her face.

'How would I know that? He said you were his number two, but he didn't tell me you were married.' She felt herself flush, fingering the string of pearls around her neck to steady her nerves.

The waiter set up the martinis and a bowl of olives on their table.

'My name's Jason,' said Melody's companion. He raised his glass to her. 'I am married, but my wife knows all about Lifestyle, and that I'm meeting you. She's at home in the USA. Is my being married important?'

'Yes, I suppose.' Melody shrugged. 'I don't do affairs with married men.'

'Is that why you agreed to meet me – because you are looking for a new lover? Daniel told me that your love life, so far, has been a disappointment.'

Melody recalled her candid conversation with Daniel and his questions the night before. 'To be honest, I haven't really *had* much of a love life. My husband Oliver, a couple of flings and two love affairs. The last one ended because the person moved. More recently, I've been seeing someone I work with, but that's about to end. It's pretty sad for a woman of my age, don't you think?'

'Well, let's see if I can help you change that. Tell me about your ex-husband.'

'Oliver? Not much to tell. He runs his own agency, and...'

'I meant in the bedroom.'

Melody laughed. 'Let's just say he was quick. His main focus was my breasts. They're probably the reason he married me. I was sixteen. He always chooses well-endowed younger women. But they're getting dangerously young the older he gets. It's a bit sick and pathetic, to be honest.'

'Well, your breasts are definitely worthy of attention. Your husband didn't make sure you were satisfied?'

'If you mean, did I have an orgasm, no. I had no idea they were even a thing until after we divorced.'

Jason pulled a pitying face, then reached to place his hand over hers. 'But now you know they *are* a "thing", as you call them.'

'Yes, well I...' She felt herself turning red again.

'You masturbate?'

Melody gulped a mouthful of the untouched martini.

He smiled. The flickering candle on the table reflected in his sable eyes. 'The driver will be back shortly. Do you want to come with me, see if we can correct some of what you have been missing?'

'Do you mean sleep together?'

'I could explain, but I think you'll find the experience more satisfying if you allow me to show you.' He offered her his hand.

Melody finished the cocktail, slipped off the stool and followed him into the Bentley.

'I'm going to ask you to wear this,' he said, holding up a silk eye mask he'd taken from his pocket.

Melody knew that this was her chance to walk away. That once she put on the mask, she was agreeing to engage with him however he wanted. She consented, allowing him to fix it in place, gasping at her own daring and wondering what the driver thought. It was a short drive; she guessed they were back at the flats on Prince of Wales Drive.

Jason guided her out of the car, up the steps of the building. 'We're going in a lift,' he said, helping her through the front door.

She heard the cage of an old-fashioned lift open. She wanted to ask him how many other women he had escorted through the building wearing a blindfold and what the neighbours thought. She paid attention to the sounds, but all she could hear were their own footsteps as he guided her along a corridor, through another door. Then the click of a lock.

When he released her arm, she raised her hands to remove the mask.

'Leave it on,' he said. 'First, do you need to use the toilet or freshen up?'

Melody hesitated. 'No… well, maybe.' She wondered what he meant by freshening up, and what she would do if he came in with her.

'I'll take you to the bathroom. Once the door closes, you can remove the mask. When you're ready, put it back on and tap the door.'

Melody removed the blindfold and caught her breath. The bathroom was huge, with a black-tiled floor and white enamel fixtures, including a shower and free-standing bath with silver trim. Elaborate mirrors reflected her movement from three of the walls. There were round, black metal hooks fastened to wooden plinths in the centre of the ceiling and above two of the mirrors. Various lengths of chain, rope and fine strips of leather hung on the back of the door. The mirrored cabinet held a metal collar and some scented oils.

Melody fingered a length of leather, then put on the eye mask. She tapped the door and waited.

'Did anything you saw in there interest you?'

Melody nodded.

'And you want to continue?' he asked. 'Will you allow me to show you how much pleasure you're capable of?'

'Yes.'

'Before we start, you'll need to choose a safe word.'

'What do you mean?'

'After I undress you, I'm going to punish you. If you want to stop, you say the safe word.' He waited for her nod, then unzipped her dress and released her breasts from the bra. 'I can see why they beguiled your ex. How about you chose *his* name for your safe word. If you want me to stop, just say "Oliver".'

Melody snorted at the irony and let out a gasp when his hand slapped her.

He removed her satin briefs and bent her over a padded bench. 'I'll begin softly, but the pressure will increase. I'm going to test your tolerance. Stay very still.'

She flinched as the strands of a leather flogger landed on her flesh. When the pressure increased, she was tempted to stop; then she remembered Daniel's instructions and concentrated on her breathing. Her butt cheeks were stinging by the time he was finished.

'Good girl. After a few sessions, you'll be able to withstand a lot more,' he said. 'Now turn round, while I help you onto the bench. Lie backwards with your hands above your head.'

Parting her legs, he strapped each of her ankles into stirrups.

With meticulous precision, he wove two lengths of plaited rope around her wrists, down each of her arms, across her breasts and torso. He secured the rope through metal rings on each side of the bench until she was completely bound and helplessly immobilised.

Melody felt her heart beating faster as the ropes were wound around securing her. Being fastened to the bench was exhilarating, stimulating her. She had never experienced such an intense climax without anyone touching her. She had no idea how long he left her tied down and when he released her, she climaxed again.

'You certainly needed that, didn't you?' he said. He guided her off the bench and back to the bathroom. 'You can freshen up and dress. The car will be here shortly.'

He leaned in, pulled her towards him and kissed her. Tracing his hands over her breasts, he whispered, 'I have so much more to teach you.'

She trembled and smiled. 'How delicious,' she said.

Four

Melody adjusted to the half-light of the evening sunset. She was surprised that it wasn't already dark when he put her in a taxi. Elated by what she had experienced, looking forward to learning more, she sighed heavily when the taxi pulled up outside her building and Charles was standing with his hands stuffed into his jacket pockets and his shoulders stooped.

'What are you doing here? Did dinner with the clients finish early?'

'It's almost nine. They had to travel back north. You should have been there. You know they only came to the agency because of you.'

'Oh, heavens, they chose us because we're a good agency. You're the Creative Director. Your campaign brought in the business.'

Charles studied her as they walked towards the front door. 'Something's happened. You look different.'

Melody smiled. 'I'm taking time for some…' She paused. 'Self-care. Something I didn't realise I needed.'

'Let *me* take care of you. Would you like a massage?'

'That's a nice offer, but not tonight.'

'What's going on? You can hardly look at me.'

Melody bit her lip. 'I think its best if we don't continue. It's too difficult to keep our personal and professional lives separate.'

Charles shook his head. 'If it's because I came to the hotel, I'm sorry, I promise that won't happen again.'

'It's not just that. We can't talk here – you'd better come in. I'll make some coffee.'

Charles, who had sprawled out on her forest green couch, sat up when she brought the cafetière through to the living room.

'I haven't made it too strong,' she said. 'I don't want to keep you awake, with all the work you've got on.'

'Don't patronise me,' he snapped.

Melody bristled; she felt guilty, but his apparent neediness aggravated her. It was only ever supposed to be fun, a fling. 'Let's not fall out. You knew this wasn't long-term. No commitment, we agreed.'

'You said we should keep things light, and I haven't made any demands of you.'

'Coming to the hotel last night, waiting outside my flat

tonight, tells me we're definitely looking for different things.'

'You're too independent, that's your problem. You're afraid of being loved.'

'Really? Well, thanks for the heads-up.' She smiled, thinking about Daniel and what she had just experienced with Jason.

'You're laughing at me because I mentioned love?'

'I'm past wanting a row or having to explain myself to any man. I respect you professionally, Charles, and we had some recreational fun, but that's all it was. Please don't make things awkward or spoil the memory of that.'

Charles poured himself another coffee from the pot and stared at her. 'Recreational fun? You make me sound like a theme park.'

'You know that's not what I meant.'

He shrugged, slurped the coffee, stood up and left without saying anything more.

Melody watched from the window as he slouched away from the building. She put on an LP, and began moving to the music, recapturing the excitement she had experienced earlier.

The following morning, the agency reception area buzzed loudly with staff voices, which stopped as soon as she arrived. One of the senior executives said, 'Someone's broken in. The studio's trashed and the campaign the creative team were working on has disappeared.'

'Where's Charles?'

The exec shook his head. 'He's not here, and he's not answering his phone. Should we call the police?'

'Thank you, everyone, but this is an internal matter. If your work area or office isn't damaged, please get on with whatever you're supposed to be doing. We have clients coming in for lunch, and we need to be professional despite what's happened.' She pointed to her secretary and the executive. 'Can you both come with me to look upstairs?'

Melody gasped when she saw the turmoil of the studio. Phones ripped out of their sockets, the typography station turned upside-down, paper, chalks and inks piled into a heap in the middle of the room. All the presentation boards for the rejected campaign were torn off the walls. The walls themselves sprayed with black, graffiti-style lettering, telling the world that Melody Wild was a witch.

'Too right I am, Charles,' she said through gritted teeth. She turned to her secretary. 'OK, can you photograph this with the Polaroid for our records? Once you've finished, ask the janitor to cover the windows, so that no one can see inside. He'll need to hire muscle to get this all fixed up. Tell him we need it done quickly, and that whoever he hires needs to keep quiet.'

Her secretary nodded and left the room.

The exec pointed at the walls. 'What's all this about? It's pretty personal. Are you alright? What about the campaign?'

Melody shook her head. 'The campaign wasn't working. I rejected it. Didn't Charles talk to you yesterday?'

'Yeah, he was furious. I didn't imagine he'd do anything like this, though.'

'Me either,' she said, and she went down to her office.

She sat back and thought about what she'd said to Charles the night before, cursing herself for playing too close to home, getting involved with someone who worked for her. She drummed her fingers on the top of the desk. She knew she had every right to call the police and report Charles, but she didn't want what had happened to get beyond the agency. While she was considering her options, the phone rang. It was Daniel.

'Now isn't a good time,' Melody said. 'Something's happened at the agency, I need to fix it.'

'I know,' he said.

'What, how?'

'I have a friend at *Campaign* HQ. We met for breakfast. There's going to be something in the diary column tomorrow.'

'How? For pity's sake, I don't believe it.'

'You'll be fine. Just ride it out. Deny, deny, deny. I assume you're looking for a new Creative Director?'

'Once I get my head over what's just happened, yeah.'

'Maybe I can help.'

'You?'

'Yeah me. I hear you had a good time last night, and I feel a little responsible for the mess you're in.'

She laughed. 'Well, yesterday *was* rather good, I have to admit. But the only one to blame for today's mess is me. I made a poor choice, and I wasn't kind.'

'And he behaved like a spoiled child. You enjoy sensory surprises, I hear. I had something planned for later, but given what's happened this morning, we'll postpone it until tomorrow.'

'I'm not sure...'

'Sure about what? You've a business to run, but that doesn't mean you don't deserve time to enjoy yourself.'

'The timing couldn't be worse, but you're right. OK, tomorrow. Thanks, Daniel.'

'My pleasure. You should expect a call later from a potential Creative Director, a woman. She's pretty special. Her name's Clodagh.'

Melody spent the rest of the day trying to calm the chaos, hurt feelings and confusion Charles had caused to her staff, especially the creative team. She phoned the local Italian restaurant and organised to take everyone for lunch at the end of the week. The janitor had taped off the windows and started on the clean-up. The clients, who'd arrived early for their lunch, had no idea that anything was wrong.

She called a staff meeting in the boardroom before they went home. 'There's going to be something about the agency in the *Campaign* diary section tomorrow. But, with your help, that new business could still be ours.' Melody looked around at her staff carefully. 'If anyone needs a chat with me, you know where I am.'

She was packing up her bag to leave when Daniel called again.

'Clodagh was busy earlier, but she's free to meet you this evening, if you want.'

'Sure, why not. Does she want to come here?'

'I thought I'd introduce you. How about The Hilton Rooftop Bar at eight?'

'Yeah, perfect.'

Melody went home, changed into a black sleeveless Yves St Laurent and booked a taxi to take her to the hotel.

'Hello again.' Jason was standing at the bar.

'Oh, hello. This isn't a coincidence, surely.'

'A person can never be too sure, when it comes to Daniel.'

'I thought I was meeting a potential new Creative, a woman.'

'You are. Daniel invited me to have a drink with him, while you two ladies got to know each other.'

Melody inclined her head. 'You know who I'm meeting? Have you met her before?'

His face remained neutral, telling her nothing.

Daniel arrived, accompanied by a tall, slim woman of

Ghanaian heritage. Melody noticed Jason and Clodagh acknowledged each other with polite smiles.

'Why don't you and Clodagh have your meeting over there, while I catch up with Jason?' Daniel suggested.

Clodagh's ebony complexion was flawless. She had long limbs, short hair, thick eyelashes and full lips. She's beautiful enough to model, Melody thought, as Clodagh slid into the chair opposite her.

Clodagh opened the portfolio she'd been carrying. 'Shall I show you what I've been working on?'

Melody spotted the gold charm dangling from the bracelet on Clodagh's wrist, engraved with the same logo as the one on Daniel's card and Jason's ring. 'Before we do that, tell me how you know Daniel and Jason.'

Clodagh gazed steadily back at Melody. 'Daniel is a business colleague. I met him in Accra. I met Jason when I was working in California.'

Melody nodded, then pointed to the portfolio. 'I'd love to see.'

As soon as she opened it, Melody could see Clodagh had a unique talent. 'Which agency are you with right now? There's no UK work here.'

'I arrived in London three months ago. Until I find somewhere to work permanently, I'm freelancing. The UK concepts I'm working on are all confidential, so I can't show them to you. But I do have an idea for the product you are hoping to pitch for.'

'Which product?'

Clodagh whispered the name of the company.

'How did you know *we* were pitching for it?'

'Daniel knew, through someone at *Campaign*.'

Melody rolled her eyes. 'How do they know everything?'

Clodagh shrugged. 'I guess that's their job. Shall I show you my ideas? I've put the presentation up in a private room. Daniel said it was urgent.'

'Daniel knows a lot more about me and my business than he ought to. OK, lead the way.'

Clodagh had just finished her presentation when two staff and a trolley full of food arrived, followed by Jason and Daniel.

Daniel looked at Melody. 'Well?'

'What else can I say but yes. The concept's amazing, Clodagh,' Melody said, noting the two men exchanging glances. 'Welcome to the agency.'

After they'd eaten, Clodagh left the hotel with Jason and Daniel took Melody back to her flat. 'Aren't you glad you came to talk with me after the fundraising dinner?' he asked, sipping the neat whisky she poured.

Melody raised her glass. 'Yes, but also concerned. I saw the charm on Clodagh's bracelet, and she left with Jason. I saw the way you both look at each other when I asked her to come and work with me... I don't want to risk another Charles situation.'

'Are you asking me whether Jason and I slept with her?'

Melody knew she sounded churlish and jealous. Clodagh was younger than she was and extremely beautiful. She nodded. 'After Charles, I want to keep my personal and private lives very separate.' Melody swallowed. 'I didn't realise I might end up working with some of your members.'

'You're not a member yet, so it's not too late. You can still hire Clodagh and not join the organisation.'

'Wait, what do you mean? I thought after you and me, and then Jason...'

'You have a selective memory when it suits you. What did I say when I helped you into the taxi?'

'That you and I would decide at the end of the summer.' Melody nodded. 'I forgot. OK, but how much does Clodagh know about me and the fact that I might join the organisation?'

'She only knows that you're looking for a Creative Director and need help to win some business. That's why nothing happened at the hotel, much as Jason and I wanted to strip you both and strap you end-to-end on that long table. Playing with you together would be quite delightful. It was tempting but, thinking of your professional reputation, we resisted.'

Melody closed her eyes and moaned, 'Stop, you're going to make me come.'

Daniel grabbed her hair and pressed her face into his crotch.

'Let's make that happen,' he said, pulling her up from the chair and leading her over to the dining table. He used his tie to blindfold her, unzipped her dress and told her to lie face-down on the wood.

The wood was cool and hard against her flesh. She listened as he searched her kitchen. Moments later she heard the scrunch of plastic wrap.

He stretched it over and under her legs, pulling them tightly together until he reached her hips. 'Arch your belly,' he said. He fed the roll of wrap under her, pulling it tightly over her buttocks, then her torso and the outside of her arms, pinning them on either side of her. When he reached her upper back, he rolled her over and continued wrapping her, stretching the sticky plastic tightly over her breasts, until he reached her shoulders.

The sensation was intense. Melody opened her mouth and flicked her tongue over her lips letting him know she wanted to receive him as he bent over her face.

'Not yet,' he whispered. He rubbed something cool on her cheeks, around her lips and then inside her mouth.

She swallowed as the cream reached the back of her throat and purred.

'You like that,' he said. 'How about this?' He trickled liquid slowly at the side of her mouth, careful not to choke her, and laughed when she made a face at the sour vinegar. He followed the vinegar with olive oil, rubbing it over her face after she tasted it then massaged it into her hair and scalp.

The plastic wrap was making her hot. She realised Daniel hadn't asked for a safe word. Melody opened her mouth to say stop when he began to cut open the wrap.

'I'm going to shower you, then take you to bed,' he told her, leading her upstairs. She was still wearing his tie over her eyes.

He showered her, massaging her body with soap, washed her hair, towel-dried her and carried her to the bed.

She spread herself open, and he took her gently until she climaxed. Then, flipping her over, he pumped her until she was limp and exhausted. She fell asleep in his arms.

Daniel was already gone when she woke. She giggled when she read the note on her bedside table. 'Very funny,' she said at the cartoon parody of the rejected advertising campaign.

Five

Melody introduced Clodagh to the creative team. Everyone responded enthusiastically to her ideas.

'This is definitely sexier,' said Sally Lemon, one of the copywriters.

Clodagh smiled modestly. 'I'm sure your input – all of your

ideas – will make it even better.'

'Thank you, Clodagh. I'm determined to get this account. As you can see, there's so much more you can do with the product than wrap bowls.' Melody blushed when saw Clodagh smile. She wondered if Clodagh and Jason had also had fun with plastic wrap last night.

The diary column in *Campaign* wasn't as bad as Melody had dreaded. No names used. The inference to an irreconcilable difference in opinion didn't bother her. Creative teams and agency chiefs often fell out and split up. At least her personal life hadn't been dragged through the mud for everyone to comment on. Oliver, for one, would certainly have relished that opportunity.

She was due to dine at a favourite Soho Brasserie with a client. 'Would you like to come too?' she asked Clodagh.

'Better not. I don't want the team to think I'm getting too much attention until we've jelled a bit more. Thanks, though.'

'You're right. They were very much hand-picked by Charles, but after what he did, they feel extremely let down. Gaining their loyalty shouldn't be too much of a problem.' She noticed Clodagh was wearing the charm bracelet again. She looked around curiously, but no one else in the agency seemed to be sporting the logo on jewellery or clothing.

Two weeks later, after winning the new business and confirming Clodagh as her Creative Director, Melody felt more confident than she had ever felt before. The Melody Wild Agency's star was rising. She enjoyed having so many people openly greeting her when she arrived at a Soho Brasserie to meet with clients for yet another lunch.

When she passed a table of four men on her way to the

washroom, she noticed one of them wearing a tie with the Lifestyle logo. It was subtle, and she wondered how many times she'd seen the logo before and not registered it. She looked around to see if Jason or Daniel were in the restaurant, but she couldn't spot them.

After she wined-and-dined her clients and prepared to leave, she looked over at the table she'd passed. Two of the men were still in the restaurant. The man with the Lifestyle tie raised a glass in her direction. She inclined her head and smiled. Moments later, one of the waiters asked her if she would like a glass of champagne, and pointed to the table where the men were sitting.

'They wondered if you'd like to join them, but the champagne is for you either way.'

Melody smiled, a tingle of excitement fluttering in her tummy. 'I will join them.'

The men stood while she walked over to the table. They stayed standing and watched her glide elegantly onto the chair the waiter had pulled out for her.

'Thank you. I'm not sure that we've met before.' She offered them her hand. 'Melody Wild, owner of The Melody Wild Agency.' Instead of a handshake, both of them bowed slightly and, in turn, brushed the top of her hand as Daniel had done. Was this a way of letting her know they were members of the organisation, assessing her to see if she recognised it? Why else had they picked her out? Then she remembered Jason's most recent comment after she dined with him two days before:

'You're going to be celebrated and recognised as a prize to be captured, if you continue like this.'

Up to that point, all the sexual and sensory experiences she'd had since meeting Daniel had been solely with him or Jason.

The length of time they restrained and teased her, demanding her to control her orgasms, had extended. The floggings with crops, whips and paddles were more intense as she expressed her desire to endure pain throughout the punishments they meted out on her. She relished in the different sensations that the rope, chains and leather harnesses offered.

The men sat on either side of her. She sipped on the champagne and felt a hand on each of her knees, pulling her legs open under the floor-length white tablecloth. As if their movements were choreographed, they moved their hands up the inside of each of her legs, until they reached her panties. She felt fingers probing her, pulling the gusset of her panties to one side.

'She's ready,' said the man with the tie.

'Lean on the table slightly and lift up your bottom,' the other man told her.

Their fingers entered her front and back passages at the same time. Holding onto the table, she groaned quietly while they moved in sync with each other until she climaxed.

Melody had learned how to control her reaction, to orgasm quietly, allowing the sensation of pleasure to run through her body. She lowered herself onto the chair again. 'How did you know?' she asked quietly.

'We weren't sure. But the way you carried yourself when you walked in – you look like a woman who knows what pleasure is. Rick, who had to leave, saw you talking with Daniel at some dinner a few weeks ago. But we're not finished with you yet.'

Melody trembled at the thought of pleasing them however they wanted her to. 'Can we meet later? I'm supposed to go back to work. I have an agency to run.'

'The longer you make us wait, the more it will hurt,' one of them said, smiling.

'I can be available after seven. Is that long enough for you to plan what I deserve? Although I should clear it with Daniel – I'm still on probation,' she laughed.

The two men exchanged looks. 'Oh, heck. We love punishing probationers, but usually it doesn't go this way round. We'd better call him, and so should you. I'm pretty certain he'll be the one seeing you later – and just so you know, we're *all* in big trouble.'

Daniel had called three times by the time Melody returned to the agency.

'What the hell?' he said.

'Sorry, I didn't realise I was doing anything wrong. *I* didn't approach *them*, even though they were wearing the logo in a public restaurant.' Her voice was bright, feigning innocence.

'Probationers are only supposed to be managed by senior members. You've so much more to experience before I'm ready to invite you to join and you're ready to decide if Lifestyle is really what you want.'

'But I *am* ready, Daniel. I want to join, commit myself.'

'OK, but there are protocols. You'll be punished in front of a group for breaking the rules, and then you'll need to be evaluated separately by two members. Are you sure you're up to these happening together, and so soon?'

'Yes,' said Melody. In less than three weeks, she'd allowed herself to explore new experiences and a lifestyle that excited her. Instead of waiting until the end of the summer, she already knew she was ready.

'When they assess you, they may expect you to participate in activities you haven't yet experienced. I have no control over that. If you stop it at any point, you'll be back on probation.

Understood?'

'Understood. I'll be fine.'

'I hope so. I'll set things up and send the car for you. The driver will give you a mask. Wear it as soon as you get it. Oh, and you'd better wear something you won't mind getting torn. Underwear, too.'

'Wait, how rough is this public punishment going to be?'

'Ah, now you're worried. Good. You have your safe word. Same rules.'

'Will you be there?'

'The whole point of the mask is so you won't know where you are, who's there or who's responsible. But I can tell you that Jason will be overseeing rather than taking part.'

She examined the dress she was wearing: an oatmeal-coloured Chanel, one of her favourites. She didn't want it spoiled, but she had a meeting at six and wouldn't have time to change before Daniel's car arrived.

'I need to pop out for half an hour,' Melody told her secretary. She took a taxi to a local boutique that sold inexpensive day wear. She chose a lime-coloured, button-up shift and a cream silk one-piece to wear under it. She was as excited as a teenager getting ready for a first date.

Six

'Here you are, madam,' said Daniel's driver as he handed her a small bag. 'Do you need help to fix it and manage your hair? A single plait usually works best with this style.'

The soft leather mask would cover her head and eyes, fitting over her nose, fastened by a zip at the back.

'Thank you,' she said, slipping it on and turning so the driver could tie her hair and fasten the zip. It felt very secure, unlike the eye masks or ties, which sometimes slipped.

When the car stopped and the driver helped her out, her arms were immediately restrained behind her by cuffs. She was escorted up some steps. She knew she wasn't at Jason's because there was no lift and only one door. It felt more like a house. A voice she didn't know told her to kneel, and to call anyone who spoke to her 'sir' or 'madam'.

'Safe word?' Jason asked.

'"Oliver", sir,' she said.

'And you are here because?'

Melody wasn't sure what to say.

'Because she's broken the rules. She's not a member – she's still on probation.' It was a woman who spoke this time.

'Is that correct?'

'Yes, sir.'

'Do you agree to be punished publicly?' the woman asked.

'Yes, madam,' Melody replied.

'Proceed,' said Jason.

She felt something cold against her neck and heard the click of a collar snapping shut. It was snug, but not too tight. She wondered if it was one of the metal collars she'd seen in Jason's bathroom.

'Stand up and step out of your shoes,' ordered the woman.

Melody wobbled slightly as she raised herself, trying to balance with her hands still secured behind her back. As soon as she stepped out of the stilettos, she felt the warm breath of whoever was standing in front of her, then the sound of scissors cutting off the buttons of her dress, followed by the straps of the one piece. Hands brushed across her flesh, tearing off the fabric until she was naked.

Melody strained, listening for voices to see if she could hear Daniel's amongst the whispers. Her ankles and legs were bound together. The rope was then tightly woven around her torso and breasts, pressing into her flesh. She yelped as her body rotated. She was suspended upside down. The blood rushed to her head as she was swung slowly back and forth.

'I'll keep watch while you all eat,' said the woman.

'Don't tease her too much,' someone said.

The woman laughed. Melody felt flicks of something soft against her exposed flesh between the layers of rope. It felt like a feather from the tickling stick Daniel had teased her with. 'Did you enjoy the finger fucking at lunchtime?'

'Yes, madam.'

'Wrong answer. You were on probation. Do you like being punished?'

'Yes, madam.'

'Have you been punished by a woman before?'

'No, madam.'

Melody felt the woman's fingers against her nipples and gasped when a metal clamp was attached to each of them.

'Don't come,' said the woman.

'Yes, madam,' she said breathily.

'Nipple clamps, good thinking,' a man's voice said. 'I'll take over.'

He opened Melody's mouth with his fingers and traced the outline of her lips. Adding yet another dimension to her experience, he inserted three fingers into her mouth. Unable to touch herself, she sucked on his fingers until the tingling sensation in her loins exploded.

'You were told to hold that,' he said.

'I'm sorry, sir.'

She tensed when she heard Jason's voice. 'Did she come?'

'Yes. No control. She's enjoying herself.'

Jason snorted. 'Let's bring her down.'

Melody was freed from the rope and the nipple clamps. The metal collar was exchanged for a leather one. Jason fastened a leash to the collar and led her across the room, where he strapped her across a padded bench.

'Remember to pace the impact. I'll signal when to stop, unless she uses her safe word.'

Melody was determined to withstand whatever was going to happen next. By the time Jason told them to stop, she realised she'd withstood almost thirty strokes, delivered with varying force. Twelve more than she'd managed last week, when Daniel whipped her. Her heart raced as she tried to control the orgasm threatening to explode.

Jason summoned her assessors. 'She's all yours for the next hour. It's your role to see if she *is* really ready for membership. You can experiment however you choose. The bell will ring when time is up, unless she uses the safe word. Thank you for doing this.'

'It's our pleasure,' said two voices in unison.

Melody recognised them: the men from the restaurant.

Melody hadn't experienced being strapped to the Saltire before. They fastened her facing away from them. Then spun her round fast. When it slowed and stopped, she was upside-down. They teased and punished her with ice, hot stones, feathers, oil, floggers and a crop. Finally, topping and tailing her, they pumped her hard with rough, coordinated movements.

'Congratulations, Melody,' one of them said when she moaned, coinciding with the bell. They released her from the cross and sat her on a chair. 'Wait here until the door closes. Then you can remove the mask and use the shower to clean yourself. Daniel will come and fetch you.'

She heard clapping as the men left, before the door closed. She reached for the zipper at the back of the mask, shook her head, and then released her hair from the plait.

She looked around and saw the equipment she had been strapped to. She hoped she would be able to play on it another time. She smiled, imagining Daniel and Jason strapping her to it, punishing her before taking her together. She was in the shower when she heard Daniel's voice congratulate and welcome her to Lifestyle.

He dried her with a thick bath sheet, combed her hair and watched her apply some of the makeup from the dresser. 'This is for you,' he said, draping a gold chain with a diamond pendant round her neck.

'It's beautiful,' she said. She leaned up to kiss him.

'You're a very special woman, Melody.'

Melody noted his tone. 'Why so serious? I thought this was a celebration. If it hadn't been for you, I would still be sleeping with Charles, putting on that fake persona you saw through. Now I feel as if I could do anything.'

'You already had confidence, but your ex diminished your sexuality and sparkle. He's a mean son of a bitch.'

'I wasted so many years wondering what I'd done wrong, why I wasn't good enough. Now I know that it wasn't me at all.'

'We should go back through. There are lots of other people here, now, who weren't part of what happened earlier. I had the driver put your change of clothes in one of the bedrooms. I'll show you where later.'

'That rope suspension was thrilling, not really a punishment.'

Daniel laughed. 'Jason thought you'd like that. We had been hoping to give you the experience at his place, but that'll have to wait. Jason is off to the USA tomorrow, to see his family and develop the organisation over there.'

'Is Jason's wife a member?'

'No, they were childhood sweethearts. She knows all about Lifestyle, but not who the members are. The experiences you enjoy aren't for her, but they share other things in common. They came to an arrangement which works for them both. Do you mind if I lead you?' he said, holding up a leather collar and harness.

'Please do,' she said, slipping off the towel.

The assembled guests applauded and cheered when Daniel appeared with Melody. He led her up onto a small podium.

'Melody has been a quick study. Her probationary period lasted just over three weeks. She has proved her commitment to our lifestyle by what she experienced and enjoyed this evening. I have invited her to become a member.'

Melody looked around at the large group of guests watching her.

Daniel lifted her arm and clipped on a gold bracelet, engraved with the organisation's logo. 'You'll also receive a personalised collar and harness, but as this all happened rather more quickly than I planned, they're not ready yet.'

The audience laughed, and Melody blushed.

'I'm sorry,' she said quietly, smiling first at Daniel and then at the two men who had got her into trouble. Her smile changed to a grimace when she caught the eye of the man standing next to Jason. It was the marketing director of a large conglomeration. She had known him since she was married to Oliver.

He smiled at her and raised his glass. 'The talented Melody Wild,' he said. 'Oliver will be delighted.'

Daniel reached over and caught Melody as she fainted.

Seven

Jason held a glass of water to her lips; she was resting on the chaise in another room of the house.

'I'm so sorry,' she said.

'It was just a panic attack. Try to relax now. You've had quite a day.'

'I should have listened to myself,' said Daniel, pacing. 'I knew getting this organised so fast was a bad idea.'

'You're not helping,' said Jason, putting his hand over Melody's as she tried to get up. 'It was all fine until Murdoch arrived. He wasn't on the guest list. I've no idea how he knew that Melody would be here.'

'And now he'll tell Oliver, and it will be all over London,' she said.

'Discretion and confidentiality are what keep everyone safe,' said Daniel. 'Including him. He'll not dare tell Oliver – he's too much to lose personally if he does.'

'He's known Oliver forever. I was really surprised when he approached us about giving one of their new products to my agency. All his other business is with Oliver's agency.'

'Could he have had a dual purpose?'

Melody nodded. 'Spying for Oliver, you mean? Feeding stuff to *Campaign*. Of course – I'm an idiot. That's how Oliver knew we were pitching for Happy Wrap, and about Charles, although I didn't think anybody had cottoned on to that mistake.'

'What's Charles's other name,' asked Jason.

'Ramirez.'

'Shit. I should have realised,' said Jason. 'He has a brother in the police.'

'Yes. George. Why, what should you have realised?' Melody demanded.

'It was George who recommended Murdoch. George was on the guest list for tonight, but he's not here. I'm sorry, Daniel, I didn't make the connection when I checked who Melody might know. Ramirez isn't a common name for London. I should have been more thorough.'

'Whatever happens, I don't regret tonight, or any of it.' Melody looked at the two men. 'Meeting you both has changed my life, who I am. If he and Oliver choose to be jerks about it, that's on them.'

'Good on you,' said Jason.

Melody rose from the chaise and opened the vanity case with her Channel dress folded inside. She removed the blanket and dressed. 'I hear you're off to the States tomorrow.'

'Yeah, you should think about an office in New York or California. Clodagh will have lots of contacts, and I'd get to see you more.'

'I like that idea. The Melody Wild Agency goes international.'

'Whoa, hold your horses, Jason. Remember our conversation yesterday?' Daniel's tone was friendly, but Melody thought she detected an undercurrent.

Jason smiled and slapped Daniel on the back. 'I warned you, you'd better not wait too long to have that conversation.'

'What's going on with you two?' she asked.

'Daniel needs to talk to you.' Jason hugged Melody and kissed the top of her head.

'Very avuncular,' she laughed, as he squeezed her into him.

'I'm going to make sure everyone is gone and the clean-up has started. Then I'll deal with Murdoch. I have to fly home in less than seven hours!'

'I'll take you home,' Daniel told Melody, when Jason had gone.

'Are you coming in to discuss whatever it is you need to talk to me about?' she asked Daniel when the Bentley arrived outside her building.

'No, I need to think some things through. I'll talk to you tomorrow morning – or rather, *this* morning. It's already two am. Sorry.'

'Have I done something wrong? Do you regret inviting me to join Lifestyle?'

'No! Absolutely not, but…' He touched her face and kissed her tenderly. 'Go in and get some rest. You may have a busy day tomorrow.'

'Always a busy day,' she smiled, waved and went inside.

The latest copy of *Campaign* was waiting on her desk when she arrived at work. Anything disclosed about last night had been too late for an article, but they'd included a line in the diary section. *'According to a private source, the Wild Agency might be a heaven-sent opportunity for people with a certain kinky disposition.'* She closed her eyes and clenched her jaw. At least she knew who was feeding them their information. She phoned Daniel.

'I've just read it,' he said. 'I have an idea.'

Two hours later, Melody was transfixed, listening to Daniel explain his idea to the owner of a multinational chain of sex shops.

'I love it,' said the owner. 'And the name's a winner. *Wild Heaven*. We can launch a range of different scents, clothing and products. How quickly could you get a campaign together?'

'I can put a team on it today, but what about the product range? Won't you need time to manufacture, design the bottles and clothing?'

'Let me worry about that. What you'll do is a teaser. We don't need to show the punters anything – just tell them something exciting is coming to market, aimed at spicing things up for all those women in the suburbs who want more than a quick how's-your-father on a Friday night.'

Melody laughed. 'Clodagh, my Creative Director, will be excited by this. She and Sally can be your lead creative team.'

'Oh, even better, a couple of chicks selling sexy products to other women. That's why I started this place. I'm a feminist.' The man smirked.

'Good for you,' said Daniel.

Melody bristled. 'My team aren't just "a couple of chicks". They're experienced professional women.'

'Yes, ma'am, that's me told. No offence intended.'

Daniel nodded. 'We need to get this to *Campaign*, discredit whatever information they think they have, especially that damn diarist.'

'She's clever. I think I admire her, actually, and I'm trying not to take it personally. I'll brief Clodagh now. Are you ready to have that conversation with me later – the one Jason was talking about last night?'

'Yes. How about dinner somewhere fancy? Will you wear the Thea Porter for me, with nothing underneath?'

Daniel was at the bar when she arrived. A half-bottle of Bollinger was open in an ice bucket.

Melody had dressed in the Thea Porter as he asked, with gold strappy stilettos and the jewellery he had given her the night before.

'Chanel Number Five,' he said, greeting her with a kiss on both cheeks.

'I remembered you said it was your favourite when you took me for afternoon tea in Harrods.'

Daniel grinned at the memory, fingering her, making her control her orgasm while the server set up the table for their tea. 'You're a wicked woman. What was it Charles wrote on the wall, a witch? I think he's right.' He signalled to the barman to fill their glasses.

'Yeah, my broomstick is ready to whisk me away any moment. What's all this about? You look tense and serious.'

'That's your fault,' he said. 'I've broken my own rules and fallen completely in love with you.' He lifted her hand and kissed it, the way he had when they first met.

Melody sipped the champagne. She didn't know what to say. The man who had told her that he was a committed singleton, with no interest in a permanent relationship, was now telling her he loved her.

'I'd even give up Lifestyle if you wanted me to. Jason would take over from me, and there are a couple of really good people here who'd bite my hand off to buy it. One of them is the woman you met last night.'

'No, oh no, you couldn't do that, I mean…' she fumbled over the words, flustered by his declaration of love and what he was willing to give up if she asked him to.

He clinked his glass against hers.

The maître d' came over to let them know their table was ready. Daniel held her hand as they walked through the restaurant.

'So, no one you know is here tonight?'

'Actually, I recognise three or four of the guests, but they're either with their wives or other people who I don't know. Why did you ask?'

'The way you held my hand, the public display of affection.'

'I want to be public about how I feel. I've never felt this way about any woman before. Certainly never considered monogamy or settling down.'

Melody felt as if their roles had reversed since that first night at the dinner. Was it really less than a month ago? Everything she'd assumed when she first saw him was the opposite of how she now felt.

'I think I love you too, Daniel,' she said. 'I say "think" because I thought I still loved Oliver, but I now know that what I feel for him isn't love. He picked me because I was young, with big tits and a virgin's naivety. He hasn't moved on. But thanks to you, I have.'

Daniel's face broke into a smile. His green eyes danced with joy, alive with tenderness and warmth.

'Once Wild Heaven is launched, can you give me a month?' Melody asked.

'For what?'

'To decide what I really want. I've only just discovered this side of me, and I'm not ready to give it up. But you told me that some of the members create exclusive groups. Could we do that?'

Daniel nodded and stroked her cheek. 'You can choose who would be part of ours, not that you know that many of the members yet.'

'Jason, when he's here. The woman who teased me and was

part of the punishment last night. And perhaps the two men who assessed me?'

'Those clowns? You can do a lot better than that, but I suppose a double act is fun.'

'Clodagh would also be fabulous, except I don't want to lose her from the agency, and I'm not doing the working-and-playing-together experience again.'

'I'll create a list. I take it you're OK if you're punished by different genders?'

Melody nodded; her tummy churned as she remembered how she'd felt, suspended and wrapped in the rope. How the woman had spoken to her, teased her and clamped her nipples. 'Yes, sir,' she said, closing her eyes as the frisson of sexual tension built inside her.

'Don't come,' he instructed her. 'Control it.'

'I can't,' said Melody, gasping.

'You'll do as I say. Remember, every day's a school day,' he said sharply. But he laughed as she came. He raised his glass. 'Cheers – here's to our future, Melody Wild.'

She clinked her glass against his.

Nine

Consent

On Saturday morning, I enjoyed the warmth of the early morning sun on my face while I ate a late breakfast in the garden. I'd been too tired and too tipsy to finish the story on Monday night, and the rest of the week had run away from me, with the book group as well as two passionate nights, making love with Peter. I fetched the Kindle and had just started re-reading chapter three when Peter arrived. He was holding a bunch of flowers.

'Sorry for interrupting your peace, but I saw these and thought of you,' he said.

'They're lovely,' I said. 'There's fresh coffee if you want some.'

He followed me into the kitchen and poured himself a coffee while I looked for a vase.

'Sorry for disturbing your reading,' he said, looking out into the garden at my lunch and the open Kindle face-down on the table.

I hugged him. 'It's a lovely surprise. I thought you were sailing with your pals from the sailing club today.'

'One's down with lurgy, the other's got a sickly baby, so...' He opened his hands. 'I remembered you said you'd be home, so I took a chance that maybe you'd like to come down to the boat with me. There's a better picnic than last weekend, and you can bring your reading too.'

I laughed at the last comment. 'Your offer is too tempting to refuse.'

We kissed, then I ran upstairs to change. When I came down, he was in the garden reading the Kindle. When he looked up at me, I could see from the expression on his face that Melody's antics in 'Wild Heaven' were not what he'd been expecting.

'Honestly, it's the first time I've read a book like that,' I said. 'My friend Heather...'

He cut me off with a hungry kiss. 'You're certainly full of surprises. I always knew there was so much more to you than you cared to share.'

'Ah, my conservative and prim work persona, you mean.'

He nodded. 'You're every man's dream of the strict librarian who lets down her hair and reveals her true nature.'

'So I'm a caricature now?'

'Not at all. You're beautiful inside and out, and *so* exciting.'

I relaxed, leaning into him. Exciting, was I? The uptight daughter of Brethren, who'd kept her emotions and passions locked inside, afraid of what would happen if, like Madame Bovary or Dorothea, she explored the world beyond the confines of what was safe and proper? I sighed contentedly while Peter stroked my hair and kissed the top of my head.

'We should go make the most of the day,' he said. 'Then later, if you'll allow me, I could teach you about knots and rope, or even…'

He picked up the roll of cling film from the counter and smiled.

I trembled slightly and nodded. Excited by the thought – the real possibility – that he was interested in exploring the world of submission and bondage with me.

'I'd consent to that,' I said, and bowed my head, holding my wrists in front of me.

About the Author

D Accord is the pen name for Liza Miles. Liza started her career in advertising and directing documentaries for television. Followed by several years in social care as an expressive arts therapist and family mediator, and as a non fiction writer Liza graduated with an MLitt in Creative Writing from Stirling University in 2022. Liza enjoys writing fiction across genres, including murder mystery, YA, children's (as Mary-Beth Mazzini) and women's fiction.

You can connect with me on:

- https://www.lizamileswriter.com
- https://www.facebook.com/lizamileswriter
- https://www.instagram.com/lizamileswriter

Subscribe to my newsletter:

- https://www.lizamileswriter.com

Also by D Accord

Milton Keynes UK
Ingram Content Group UK Ltd.
UKHW031123081124
450926UK00001B/24

9 798224 010769